Ain't No Fairytale Love in The

Hood

Part One

A.C. Irving

DEDICATION

A wise woman once told me that as soon as you're up to something great the devil will send EVERYTHING to try and distract you. *Woosah*! From the day I signed my first contract, I've faced a few roadblocks. However, I stayed down and did not let it stop me. Now, I would like to dedicate my very first book of many more to come to myself! I DID IT!

THANK YOU

My thanks will be to God first and always! I know with him all things are possible. Secondly, to my children, my life, thank you for your patience. Mommy loves you so much and we're on our way up from here. To each of my friends that helped me though this journey, I acknowledge you all as family from here on. Thank you for every time you gave me feedback on an email. For the patience you guys had with me when my mind constantly changed and I asked for advice on stories. Thank you for our late nights up on the phone figuring things out and for the constant reminders to never give up, stay focused, and that I'm doing great! THANK YOU! And last but certainly never the least, TO MY FAMILY! (From Amityville to Wyandanch

everybody Jones, bricksup) THIS IS JUST THE
BEGINNING!

A NOTE FROM
THE AUTHOR A.C.

To all of my fans and my pretty little readers, I would like to truly say THANK YOU! For every follow, every review, every page turned, I appreciate your time and your desire to read more. If you enjoy this story, I look forward to releasing many more that will take your breath away and add to your book collection! Follow me on Instagram @pr3ttylittlewriter_ to read some of my short stories outside of my novels. I'm also on Twitter, as sometimes I write random Twitter tales. Follow me there as well @prettywriterAC. You can also add me on Facebook at A.C. Irving to join my readers group! I look forward to this journey of writing and appreciate each of you who will take this ride with me! Thanks once again

for all of your support.

- A.C. Irving

INTRODUCING KIMBERLY CARTER

Kimberly Carter was ten years old when her mother passed away from "being sick." This was all she would say whenever someone asked. . . she never went into detail. At the age of 32, her mother Claire Carter, was diagnosed with AIDS, which took her life in less than one year. Kim watched the disease take over her mother's body like cancer over a course of months. So many times, Kim wished she had the money to allow her mother the care she needed. So many times, she wished she could save her life.

Growing up, it was just her and her mother for most of her young life, living in a small basement apartment located in Hempstead, Long Island. Kimberly never met any outside family. Her mother was all she knew. She never met her father, as he was nowhere to be found when her mom died, forcing Kim to become a foster child. During her first year under state supervision, Kim bounced from home to home. Each family she lived with became progressively worse. The abuse was always too much for Kimberly to bare and she would lash out, resulting in her removal from the home. The parents often reported her as violent and disobedient, while never mentioning their abusive ways.

Whenever the agency was unable to find another family to place her with right away, she would stay in group homes with hundreds of other young girls. Sometimes the group homes were worse than being with the families, but either way she wanted out. So many hours she would hide under tables and in closets and just wish she could get inside of herself and disappear. When it was time for her to be moved to another house full of strangers that they called her family, she would throw tantrums. The agency never cared. There were times when the police were involved, and they physically escorted her out of the group home. After a while she gave up fighting them. She went into a shell and lived a life that was consumed by their rules.

At almost 12 years old she was finally placed with a permanent foster family in Canarsie, Brooklyn. It was here that she met her first ever best friend Toya.

CHAPTER ONE

Kim smiled as she thought about the day that she met her best friend. It was a hot July day and school was out for the summer. All of the kids from the building were outside playing in the complex park which they called the "backyard." It was more like a huge circle in the middle of the complex but it could have been a backyard if it were a house instead of a building. In the circle there was a raggedy playground but the kids made the best of it. They made up their own versions of games from "shark on the slide" to "knick or knock" on people's apartment doors, where they would knock and then run before someone would answer the door. The backyard was the place where they had all the fun.

Kim was the new kid in the "yard" and she stood out like a sore thumb. She had never lived in or visited Brooklyn before. So much was different for Kim here. She wasn't used to being around so many kids in the same area freely. It was almost as if they were a little complex crew. She was the only child with no family that she'd known of aside from her mother. She had never made any real friends in school or at home in the neighborhood due to her constant instability in the system. She never made any friends in the group home and thought of it more as a prison. Her foster families rarely gave her the same privileges as their real kids. Because of this, she did not make friends with them either.

She became used to being alone. What she did like about Brooklyn was the fast pace. What she didn't like were the people, and the people didn't like her either. You would have thought Kim had an "about me" summary on her forehead the way all of the kids swore that they knew her. They automatically assumed that she thought she was better than others because of where she was from and the way she avoided the other kids. The truth was Kim just wanted to be left alone. She missed her mother more than anything in the world. These Brooklyn kids made it harder for her in ways that were unimaginable. They were so insensitive at times that they would use her mother's way of death as a means to tease her. She learned not to let words bother her but when her mom was mentioned, it touched her heart. These young Brooklyn chicks were mean as hell.

Kim was on one of the swings, thinking about how much her life had changed since her mom passed away when a girl much bigger than her started to tease her.

"Ewww, now we can't use the swing cootie girl," said the girl.

Kim knew she was referring to her mother's sickness. One thing she hated about the foster care system was that everywhere you went everyone knew your business. There were neither secrets nor privacy in her life. Kim ignored the girl's comment. She was upset but she wasn't going to let the bully see that. She didn't want to get into any more fights because she knew her foster parents would blame her and tell her how much of a trouble maker she was. That's how every situation would play out when she got into anything. Kim hated this shit. She looked up at the girl and noticed that it was the yard's bully, Sasha. Kim had watched her a few times before, bullying other little girls off the swings, slides, and sometimes even out of their ice cream money. She knew it was only a matter of time before Sasha tried her too.

"Oh, so you're deaf and dumb huh cootie girl?" Asked Sasha, laughing and pointing now. Kim looked around and saw that all eyes were watching, the kids were realizing that Sasha had another victim. *"God, please let this girl leave me alone"* Kim thought to herself as she closed her eyes and took a deep breath. Kim had always prayed to God since her mom left. She felt like he was the only one she had in her corner and he always listened. This time he wasn't listening fast enough. . .

"Awww, you're gonna cry now?" said Sasha. "Cry baby, cry baby!"

She was laughing even harder now and all of the kids were forming a crowd around them. This pushed Kim's buttons. Sasha was deliberately trying to embarrass her. Kim stood up and everyone grew quiet, not sure of what was going to happen next. Sasha was a little surprised but still stood her ground.

"Leave me the fuck alone Sasha," Kim said calmly giving her a fair warning. Sasha was not backing down.

"Make me," she responded with her finger in Kim's face. Kim lost it. She wasn't in the mood and she knew if she didn't make an example out of Sasha's big ass, she would always bother her and others would think they could too.

"Punk bit-", Sasha started to say before Kim punched her right in her mouth with a right hook. Sasha stumbled backwards and grabbed her mouth with a confused look on her face. She wasn't expecting this at all. Kim gave her no time to defend herself. Sasha was much bigger and Kim wanted to get the best of her. Kim followed up with a left jab and another right hook, hitting Sasha in the lip and eye. Blood started falling from Sasha's mouth. This amped Kim up and she now had her hands up as if she was in a boxing rink, jumping back and forth on her feet. She was about to give Sasha the business. Sasha was embarrassed. She couldn't let this new girl beat her up in her own hometown in front of everyone. She swung with her hardest and she missed. Before she realized she had missed, Kim hit her two more times and this time Sasha fell. The whole yard filled with "oohh's" and "aahh's" when Kim jumped on top of her and wouldn't stop punching. She heard Sasha screaming, she felt the blood on her hands, but she couldn't stop. *"I told this bitch not to bother me,"* Kim thought to herself... *"now she's getting fucked up."*

Everyone watching was in shock. . . the big neighborhood bully was screaming for mercy. They must have all felt that she deserved it because no one stopped Kim or tried to help as she beat on Sasha.

"My name is Kim bitch and I don't have no fucking cooties!" That was the last thing Kim said to Sasha before she spat on her and got up to go inside. She was over this whole day. Kim was so angry that she allowed Sasha to make her snap and she just knew that her foster parents were going to hear about it from her foster siblings. Kim was tired of getting into trouble and then being blamed for starting things when she tried her very best to avoid people and stay out of the way. She just couldn't win for losing. "Yo, wait up" said a soft voice as Kim was walking away. She turned around confused as to who could be talking to her.

"Chill out Mike Tyson. I don't want no problems," the girl said jokingly as she could see Kim was still in "ass whoop mode." Kim laughed a little before responding, "I ain't no Mike Tyson and I don't like to fight," she said to the mysterious pretty girl. She was chocolate with a round face and head full of long braids and beads. "I'm Toya," she said as she reached her hand out. "I'm Kimberly," Kim said reaching her hand out also. "I know, and you ain't got no cooties," Toya said laughing. "I like you, you ain't no punk bitch and you can fight. I know you said you don't like to but you gone have to fight a lot being out here in Brooklyn, especially since you're pretty and got hair." Toya's words made Kim giggle. This was true. Kim always had issues with the other girls in the group home either over her hair or her thinking she's too pretty just because she was confident...true jealousy and envy.

"Thank you, that bitch had it coming. I only fight when people enter my personal space but other than that I'm cool and I don't bother nobody," Kim said to Toya.

"I like that. We gone be friends Kimberly, good friends. Can I call you Kim?" Toya asked with a big smile.

Kim was confused and flattered at the same time. Someone actually wanted to be her friend and she couldn't believe it. She had no real family, kids thought she had the "cooties," she did not have as much as the other kids and none of that mattered to Toya. Kim felt it in her heart that Toya's words were sincere.

"Yeah, you can call me Kim." she answered.

"Good. Come on, imma walk you to your apartment so I can tell Mrs. Shirley the truth. It wasn't your fault and Sasha was picking on you. I don't want you to get in any trouble, I already know how it goes with Mrs. Shirley," Toya said as she led the way. Toya even knew about her foster family situation and did not judge her. Kim wanted to cry. She had finally met someone who was just nice to her. She looked up to the sky and smiled. She knew that Toya was sent from God. All she ever prayed for sometimes was a simple sister so she wouldn't have to go through life alone.

From that day forward Toya and Kimberly were BEST FRIENDS. Very rarely would you see one without the other. They became so close as adults, strangers would often think that they were lesbians. They did everything together, from skipping school to meeting up with niggas. They even went on double-dates, and experienced their first kisses while they were together.

Now it was fucking Kim's head up something terrible to hold her dead friend's body in her arms. She couldn't help but feel like it should've been her instead. "We ride together, we supposed to die together T," Kim cried. She cried her eyes out over her friend while rocking back and forth… she just couldn't believe it. A part of her was gone, the best part of her at that. *Who was she supposed to share everything with now? Who was she going to shut down parties with now? Who was going to listen to her secrets without judging her now? Who was going to be the godmother of her first child that she just found out hours ago she was pregnant with?*

So many thoughts and questions ran through Kim's mind as memories of her and Toya played over and over in her head. She thought about all of the times they laughed together, all of the times they fought together, and all of the times they cried together. They shared so much.

All she could do was cry. She just didn't know how she was going to live life without her sister. Knowing that Toya's death was personal is what hurt Kim the most. She knew who did it and she knew why. She just wasn't ready to accept that this was fate. She thought they would have had just a little more time. Kim knew that it was time to finally end this shit. She could either keep running or face the motherfuckers who did this, even if it meant that she had to face them alone. Kim wanted revenge for her best friend, and she was going to get it. Toya was her heart and she was going to get the bastards who took her life away from her.

She thought about their last few hours together. They were supposed to meet back up and get ready to leave. She wished she had more time. The last time she felt this empty was when her mom died. She knew that she had to shake it off before she spiraled into another depression.

Going through so much as a child, Kim learned to bury her feelings and emotions. She needed to be externally hard at all times because she knew how soft her heart was and the damage the pain could do to it. If she allowed her emotions to take over, she'd probably have a nervous breakdown.

She mourned for her friend for a few more minutes and then told herself that she would bury this pain with everything else. She took a deep breath and looked down at Toya. She was still beautiful even with a bullet between her eyes. It angered Kim to know that this was the way they took her out. They showed no mercy and no love. She closed her eyes, wishing that she could put her hands on the people who were responsible for this right then and there. She was going to miss her friend so much. She rocked back and forth holding Toya's head in her lap as she looked around the apartment. Everything was in place, there was no sign of a struggle, no forced entry, nothing. Kim knew who sent the hit out but had no idea how they were able to carry out the task so smoothly.

She placed her hand on her head as she tried to think, and figure shit out. She didn't know how safe she would be if she stayed in Toya's apartment, but she knew that she had to get help. She was the one responsible for finding Toya's body and this put her in a bad position. She knew that if she was the one who called the cops, she would be asking for them to get into her business, and she was already into enough illegal shit. The shit she was into is what led to Toya's death in the first place. But how could she just leave her friend? Even if she called the police and left, her fingerprints were all over the apartment. *Fuck it*, she said to herself *I'll just call these pigs and wait.*

She got up and walked to Toya's bedroom. This was so different now that Toya was gone. She felt like she was walking through a stranger's hallway. No presence of Toya was around. She found an extra sheet in one of her closets and used it to cover her friend's body after giving her a kiss on the cheek. She took a deep breath and picked up the phone to dial 911.

"911 what is your emergency?" asked the phone operator.

"I need to report a murder," Kim responded while looking at the sheet covering Toya's body. She stayed on the phone with the operator for about six minutes answering all of her questions, which seemed like they'd never end. She hung up after the operator finally assured her that an ambulance was on its way.

It was spooky for Kim to sit in her friend's house with her lifeless body just lying on the floor. They were just together, alive and breathing in this same room, planning to leave the state for good. All she could do now was just keep wishing that she had more time. She was going to wait until they were settled in their new places to tell her about the baby. "*Oh shit! The baby*," Kim thought to herself.   She was a few hours into knowing that she was just about eight weeks pregnant. This had been the least of her worries and concerns since she discovered the death of her friend. Finding out that she was pregnant was bittersweet for Kim. She knew for her own safety that there was no way that the father of this child could be in their lives. Sometimes she thought if he actually knew it would change things but then she would always remember, *a baby don't keep no nigga.* She'd never had an abortion before, although she did think about it. She always dreamed of having kids after marriage and the man she was pregnant by was definitely not husband material. She was only supposed to have fun with him and things got out of line. She liked him a lot and she once thought she loved him but she knew that he wasn't the one for her. Leaving the state was supposed to be Toya and Kim's way out of this shit they had gotten themselves involved in, so they thought.

It took the cops about forty-five minutes to get to Toya's apartment. This was regular shit in the hood to Kim. If they didn't know Toya was dead already, they probably would have taken even longer.

The police arrived at Toya's apartment before the ambulance did. They were always ready to arrest people before they could even provide medical attention.

"Hi, did you report a murder?" Asked the first officer that came to the door. Kim looked him up and down. He was chubby and looked like he would rather have been somewhere else eating donuts. She looked at his name tag before answering, "Yes, Officer Smith, I…I did."

Kim stuttered a little, she was nervous, but it was too late. They were already there.

"So, what happened?" asked the officer as he pulled out his notepad and pen ready to jot down Kim's answers.

"I came over to my friend's house and she was…" Kim stopped in the middle of her sentence and fought back tears, ". . . she was dead."

She felt the words touch her soul as they left her mouth.

"How did you get in?" the officer asked Kim.

"I have a key, this is my second home," Kim felt her words again. This was indeed her second home, and now it would never be the same again.

"And could you tell me the victim's name and how long you've known her for? And does she have any other family?" The officer asked.

"Her name is Toya Richards… I've known her most of my life, over 15 years now. Yes, she has family. Her mother's name is Margaret Richards and her number is 718-515-4307."

The cop wrote down everything Kim said in his notepad.

"Hi, I'm sorry I didn't get your name," a pretty white lady with a suit on walked over to Kim interrupting her and the police officer's conversation. Kim could tell that she was definitely a detective or off duty cop. "Well, that's because no one asked for my name…miss… I'm sorry what is *your* name?"

Kim was being sarcastic on purpose. She despised the police. She planned on answering basic questions for the officers, but she did not want to speak to any detectives. The detective sensed her attitude but still stayed polite. In her line of work, she was used to this.

"I am Detective Julia White and I will be working on this case along with my partner, Detective Dave Dawson. He's still getting a look around the place."

Detective White reached her hand out to shake Kim's, but Kim did not return the gesture.

"Well, it's nice to meet you Detective White. I'm Kimberly Carter. I don't think I would be much help to you in this case, but I do wish the motherfuckers responsible are brought to justice whether it's by law or by fate. Everything I know I've already told the officer." Kim turned to walk off.

"Wait, wait, Ms. Carter please! I have a few questions. I know you're probably upset about your friend right now and the last thing you want to do is talk to detectives, but you actually could be more help than you think."

Detective White tried to stop Kim from walking away. Kim turned around now facing the pretty detective. She decided to engage in conversation with the detective, "And how is that detective? I'm listening."

She didn't want to seem like she was hiding anything, so she allowed her to ask questions. "Well first of all, I heard you tell Officer Smith that this is like your second home and you've known the victim for over 15 years now," the detective stated.

"That's correct, and?" Kim replied wanting to know what she was hinting at.

"Well, it sounds like you must have been really close with Ms. Richards. Do you have any idea who would have wanted to hurt her? Or what she might have been into that could have led to this? She was shot in the face Ms. Carter. This seems like a vengeance or personal murder. Is there anything that you could think of that could help figure out who did it?" Detective White asked Kim as if she knew she had an answer.

"No ma'am, I honestly do not. My friend was a loving person . . . She had no known enemies that I could think of."

Kim lied. She knew exactly who would have wanted to hurt Toya, but she knew that she could never tell the police. She wanted to handle the murderers herself and she knew that if the cops found out the truth, she would be under the jail with them.

"Well, did she have any jealous ex boyfriends? Any new men she'd met? Can you give me anything?" Detective White was still trying to get any information out of Kim that she could.

"I'll tell you what detective, you can give me your card and if I can think of anything while I'm home crying over my slain sister I will give you a call," Kim said sarcastically. She'd had enough of talking to the detective. She had no information to share with them and the cops wouldn't be able to help her if she did. Detective White tried to maintain her pleasant facial expression as she handed Kim her card.

"Thank you," Kim said as she snatched the card and walked back into the living room.

Kim's mind went blank. She lost her friend and now detectives were acting like they knew something or wanted to know more. She watched as the paramedics carried her sister's body out in a body bag and she felt sick to her stomach. The next time she would be able to see her friend would be in a casket. And that was if she even stayed alive long enough to make the funeral. She knew that the same people who had killed Toya was after her too.

Kim looked down at the detective's card, *y'all couldn't help me if I wanted you to,* Kim thought to herself. She knew that there was no way she could snitch. That was against every rule of life where she was from. *If you do the crime you pay the fine.* Kim's fine was losing her sister; she wished it was a simple ticket she could pay off. She knew that by them killing Toya, it was to show her that she and Toya had fucked with the wrong people. Little did they know, killing Toya only woke up the monster that was always in Kim.

Detective White walked over to her partner Detective Dawson, "She knows something, I'm telling you."

Detective Dawson looked over at Kim and then back at his partner, "Are you sure Julia? Remember what happened last time you accused the family of a victim."

Detective Dawson reminded his partner of their last case. She had accused a victim's sister of knowing her killer and not coming forward. She failed to prove this, and she was sued and suspended without pay for weeks. "Oh, come on! Don't bullshit me Dave! We both know why that case fell apart. I'm telling you this time, I *feel* it! She knows something and she doesn't want to talk!"

Detective White spoke surely of her allegations against Kim. She walked over to Kim one last time before heading out the door, "You know Ms. Carter, it's standard procedure that we tell anyone involved or anyone that is a witness to a murder that it would be best if you didn't leave the state or the country until we have more information on what's going on. I'm sure you don't have any reason to flea town or anything of that sort, right? But it is my job to let you know," Detective White stated as she walked away. Kim watched her leave as her anger caused her blood to boil.

CHAPTER TWO

Kim left Toya's apartment cold and nervous. It was as if there was no more life left in her, she was just a walking, talking body. She knew it would be stupid of her to go home right away. It would have been too emotional for one and she was sure that it was not safe right now.

"Damn, where the fuck could I go?" she thought to herself trying to weigh out her options. She checked her pockets and found only one crumbled $100 bill. If she tried to get a hotel room for the night, she would be completely broke, the next day with no money to eat.

"Fuck!" she said out loud. Her eyes watered up thinking about how alone she really was in life. Toya was almost all she had. She knew everything about her, and she shared all her secrets with her. She shook the thoughts of Toya out of her mind remembering that for right now she needed to bury her emotions.

A thought clicked in her head that she couldn't believe didn't click sooner. *"Q!"* she said out loud. She could always call on Q. She pulled out her Blackberry with relief of having someone to call. She hesitated before she called Q and her mind wandered back to Toya. How was she going to explain this shit to Q? She decided she'd figure that out later as she called him. She had to get off of these streets.

The phone rang twice and then it went to voicemail. She called again and it did the same thing. *"Come on nigga don't let ya shit be dead right now, please,"* Kim said as she called him again. This time he picked up on the first ring.

"What's up KP?" he answered with excitement in his voice. He had given Kim this nick name from the cartoon *Kim Possible* because he felt like she was always trying to do it all. He liked that about her though.

"I need you Q," Kim said with immense pain apparent from her words. Q knew something was wrong right away from her tone of voice. He knew Kim too well and they were always able to joke no matter what mood she was in. She had always told him in the pass that she loved calling him when she was upset because he knew how to put her in a better mood. This Kim on the phone was different and he could feel it.

"Yo, what's wrong? Where you at?" Q asked, ready to be right there.

"I'm at our spot by T's..." Kim closed her eyes as she said this and paused.

When she said our, she was referring to her, him, and Toya. Their favorite spot was this little pizza joint named Big Homie's. They served the best pizza in town and they were black owned. "I'm on my way," was all Q said before he hung up the phone.

Kim started thinking about how close her, Toya and Q were. It seemed like thoughts of Toya were everywhere; she didn't know how she was going to stay strong.

Kim threw her hoodie over her head and started making her way to Big Homie's to meet Q. Walking down these Brooklyn streets brought so many memories back to Kim. She smiled as she thought about Q and how she could always count on him.

Now, Q was Kim's "favorite ex" as Toya would always joke. His name was Qazir Jones, but everyone called him Q at his request. He was 5'9 and he had pretty smooth dark chocolate skin. Q always looked like he was shining. He rocked a dark Caesar and had low, thick waves. His hair made him look mixed. His eyes were too pretty for a man. They were almond-shaped and naturally low as if he was always high. His eye lashes were thick and curly, the kind that most females wished they had. His smile could light up a room with his pearly white teeth. Q was truly mesmerizing.

Kim and Q were together for four long years before they decided to split ways. There was no bad blood between them and in fact, they always remained friends afterwards, best friends really. Their relationship ended painfully for the both of them because all they really wanted was to be together. Unfortunately, their situation was like a right person, wrong timing type of thing. They were young and still living life. They knew they couldn't love each other the way they wanted to at the time.

Kim started thinking about the first time Q ever made a move on her, she remembered this day like it was yesterday. It was a hot summer day in the middle of August and they were out at a block party in Sunset Park. Brooklyn block parties were always flooded with people of all ages.

Kim had really grown to love Brooklyn, so much changed as she grew older. She loved the hood. She loved the vibes and she even started to love the people. She remembered she was wearing a tight-fitted jersey dress from one of her favorite basketball teams, the L.A. Lakers. It was yellow, white, and purple and she complimented it with a fresh pair of yellow and white air maxes. Her hair was in a slicked-down, swoop ponytail to the side and her bamboo earrings and thick coated lip gloss made it pop. She and Toya were two of the baddest on the block. Toya wore a figure fitting, FILA jumpsuit jean dress with a blue and yellow FILA crop top underneath. She had on a fresh pair of all-white, high top FILAs to match. Her long thick hair was blown out and blowing in the wind that came and went.

Kim remembers the song "Hey Ma" by Cameron was playing and everybody was blazed, having a great time. Kim and Toya were sitting on the hood of someone's car smoking a blunt when Q and his homeboys came over to say what's up. Q had some fine ass friends and most of them were always from out of town. They would only come around on occasions. This specific day, one of his homeboys tried to holla at Kim.

Q usually never brought his friends around Kim and Toya, but they were out at a party.

"What's good with you beautiful?" Q's fine friend asked Kim. Kim looked him up and down and thought he looked good. He was a little shorter than she liked but he was handsome, and he noticed her beauty.

"Ain't shit good with her nigga, she's mine," Q said to his friend with a serious face and tone. He didn't even give Kim a chance to answer for herself and now she was lost for words. That was the first time she ever saw Q show his true feelings for her. They flirted every now and then, but their relationship was always great as friends. Q made his point to his friend seriously and simple, Kim was off limits.

Kim started smiling thinking about how Q's manliness made her feel that day. Toya looked at Kim and Kim looked at Toya, they both were thinking the same thing, *"like okay Q since when?"* This made Kim miss Toya even more; they were always on the same page no matter what the situation was. They were the type of friends where if they thought you were lying to them, they were tapping each other on the low like *this motherfucker.* Their bond was deeper than sisterhood.

None of Q's friends looked Kim and Toya's way for the rest of the party. They did their own thing and were sure to hit on anyone else but them. Kim spotted Q at one of the many grills that were fired up throughout the block. Anything that could be grilled was definitely being grilled, with the strong aroma of lit charcoal in the air.

"What's up? What you gettin'?" she asked Q already knowing he was probably getting jerk chicken with sweet sauce. That was one of his favorites off the grill.

"You know me baby, jerk chicken with the sauce kickin," Q laughed at his own corny rhyme. Kim giggled with him; she admired his sense of humor, but she wanted to get to the point. "So, I'm yours now huh?" she asked him straight up with a serious but soft tone.

"You've been mine Kim and you know that. I don't care about them other niggas you play around with but ain't none of *MY* niggas crossing that line," Q hit himself on the chest when he emphasized the word *my*.

He smiled when he said this, but he meant every word. Kim was flattered but confused, "So what the fuck does that mean Q? Cause if it's like that then imma start slapping every thirsty ass hoe I see looking your way." Kim thought she was making a valid point to Q.

"I don't give a fuck about these hoes Kim! Shit, I'll slap one of 'em for you!" Q was dead ass. He was young having fun and none of these girls around mattered to him. Kim was awestruck, she had niggas wanting her all the time, but Q made it known what it really was with him. Kim had a huge smile on her face that made her look even more like a baby.

"So, we official now?" she asked sarcastically as she rubbed Q's face.

"We official baby," he said in a sweet funny voice. They both laughed and stared at each other. They were young, Kim was 16 and Q was 18 but they couldn't deny their love for each other.

"Let me rock ya chain so these bitches know what's up," Kim said in a jokingly ghetto voice. Q took off his diamond cut Q chain and placed it around Kim's neck. This was the first chain he'd ever bought for himself and he never let anyone else wear it, especially no females. Kim was the first.

"You stuntin' like daddy now," Q joked as he admired his chain on Kim's neck. *It compliments her sexy ass just right* he thought as he looked her up and down. They tongue kissed each other deeply before heading back with their friends.

Kim couldn't help but to smile thinking about this day. When she arrived at Big Homie's Pizza Place it was busy as always. There was never a dull moment in Brooklyn and definitely not at a pizza joint. She ordered two middle Sicilian slices and sat in the corner where they always sat when they came there. They'd been going to Big Homie's for years and for some reason, no matter how busy they were, their spot in the corner was always open.

Maybe people just didn't like being in the corner, they wanted to look out the window and see the busy Brooklyn streets, Kim thought to herself. *Who knows?*

As Kim sat down with her pizza, she looked at it and couldn't eat it. Her stomach was growling, and she knew her body had to be hungry now that it was feeding for two but, she couldn't eat. If she had an appetite, she couldn't feel it.

After about ten minutes of trying to eat, she gave up and grabbed a takeout box. She sat and waited for Q's call nervously. She didn't know how she was going to tell him about Toya. She was just as much his sister as she was Kim's. Toya was the one that linked them together. Kim knew once he found out about this shit, he was going to want something touched, and she didn't have the heart to tell him the truth behind it all.

One thing she kept away from Q was her and Toya's street life. He was a street nigga himself and she never wanted to mix him up in her business. She didn't want him to know anything, and she damn sure didn't want him to get involved. She knew Q wouldn't accept any of the shit they were into, but she also knew that he would protect them both, no matter what. Q was like Kim's secret weapon. She never wanted to bring him out unless it was necessary, and now that the necessity was warranted, it was tearing her up. She knew Q could hold his own but these people who were after them were no joke. *What if it ended all bad?* She thought to herself. That would be two deaths on her hands and heart; she knew she couldn't handle that.

Kim thought about the day that Toya first introduced her to Q. She was fourteen and Toya was turning fifteen. She asked Momma Margaret if her and some friends could go to Coney Island to celebrate. She begged and pleaded with Momma to let them go alone until she gave in.

Momma Margaret was Toya's mom, but everyone called her Momma. She was respected in the neighborhood and Ms. Shirley never questioned her when it came to Kim. She was very strict and allowing them to go out alone was rare. She always gave in to Toya when she gave her that puppy dog face.

"Girl we gone have mad fun! I invited my best friend Q and his friends, and I told Shantae to come. I don't know if she's bringing anybody."

Toya was hype! She'd never been to Coney Island before and she'd always heard about how much fun it was. Kim rolled her eyes. She didn't really like Shantae, but she knew that was Toya's home girl. For some reason she just didn't get a good feeling from her.

"Now you know I don't like ya ghetto ass friend," Kim said laughing but being serious.

"I know, I know but you love me, so you gone tune her ass out, plus she supposed to know some niggas out that way that we gone have meet us there," Toya winked at Kim. She knew her friend was a fast ass and liked the thought of meeting new boys.

"Now you know damn well we don't want the same type of niggas as Shantae. Girl you must be *extra* high today," Kim and Toya both laughed.

Shantae was 16 and she'd already made a bad name for herself in their hometown. She was known for having threesomes and even letting four niggas at once run a train on her. Toya never witnessed this and Shantae swore it wasn't true, so she never judged her. She did know that Shantae never had standards. She was always seen with any man that would look her way.

"Listen Kim, we finna have a good time. I invited the bitch 'cause she's cool as hell and you know that. Now fuck her, let's get our outfits ready. My friend Q be having some fine ass friends with him anyway, so shit, if Shantae joints ain't looking too right we got options."

They both busted out laughing again. They were young and just trying to have fun. The train ride to Coney Island was awkward for Kim. She was trying her hardest to ignore Shantae but it seemed like everything she did was irking her nerves. She knew it wasn't purposely and it was only because she didn't like her, so she tuned her out for the sake of her friend's birthday.

"Girl wait till you see these niggas! They fine as hell!" Shantae told Toya while she was smacking her gum.

"I hope so Tae 'cause them last niggas was a mess," Toya busted out laughing as she gave Kim a high five. This was something Kim could agree with.

"Oh whatever! That was only one time," Shantae answered with a playful attitude.

"Shit, if Q's niggas are fine then I won't have to call mine," Shantae laughed out loud as she patted her weave trying to ease an itch on her scalp without messing it up.

Kim thought about Q. He was all Toya talked about sometimes, but it took a while for her to meet him. Toya told Kim that sometimes he would visit his grandma out of town for weeks and that's why he wasn't always around. She was ready to meet this mystery man that shared some of her friend's heart.

When they got off the train to head to Coney Island, a group of young boys was standing around like they were waiting to hit on pretty girls. Kim locked eyes with one of them and looked him up and down. He was light-skinned with a low Caesar, was fine to her and she wanted him right away.

After staring at each other for about 30 seconds, the boy started smiling and pointing over towards them. *Oh shit*, Kim said to herself. *Don't tell me these are the niggas we're meeting up with*. Just when Kim was going to turn around and ask Toya about these men, she started calling her name.

"Kim! Come here, meet Q." Toya had a big ass smile on her face as she waved her friend over. Kim felt like her mouth dropped when she saw Q. He was even finer than the man she had just locked eyes with, and she set a goal to get his number.

"Q, this is my best friend Kim. Kim, this is my best, best friend Q," Toya laughed.

"It's nice to meet you Kim. I've heard so much about you," Q smiled as he shook Kim's hand. He could tell she was admiring his looks and she liked what she saw. It was written all over her face.

Kim snapped out of it and stopped daydreaming about lying in bed with Q as she shook his hand back.

"Well, I hope it was all good things," Kim smiled as she answered him back.

"Not as good as you look," Q flirted with Kim as he turned her around by her hand. Kim was blushing and didn't mind the flattering, she turned around for him smiling before she started laughing.

"Alright now y'all, cut it out. I ain't tryna be no damn matchmaker," Toya joked as she took Kim's hand from Q. Everyone laughed at her joke.

"I don't think I'm gonna need your help for that sis," Q joked back.

"Where's the rest of the crew?" Toya asked Q changing the topic.

"They're right over there. They were using the bathroom since y'all were taking forever to get here," Q nagged at Toya playfully.

"Blame the train!" She shot back.

Q called for his friends to come over so he could introduce them. Kim was surprised to see the man she was undressing with her eyes before was there with Q. She felt a little funny knowing that she was attracted to them both. She never usually messed with guys that were friends, but she didn't think so badly of it either. *My pussy, my rules* she thought to herself as she smiled at Q's friend.

After everyone exchanged hellos and met, they were off to the amusement park. Ride after ride everyone was having a good time.

"Goldfish! Goldfish! Come win a goldfish," an older carnie was yelling out trying to attract people to his stand.

"Hey, hey, let's go try that. I always wanted a fish," Kim told Toya. Toya laughed but it was true. Kim always wanted pets growing up but she was never allowed.

After three attempts of trying to keep her spray gun straight in the game and make it to the top first, she lost.

"Goddammit!" she yelled out.

"It's ok Kim. It would've died before we made it back home anyway," Toya laughed but she was trying to cheer her friend up.

"Oh, shut up," Kim said as she let out a giggle. She wasn't mad about not winning the fish. She wanted it but what she wanted even more was to win, she hated losing at anything.

"Don't worry pretty, I got you," Q said as he walked over to the man and paid for a round. He won the game on the first try and played three times winning Kim three fish.

"I got you a fish for every time you lost," Q smiled as he handed Kim the goldfish in a sandwich bag. She laughed so hard she felt rude.

"Oh my gosh! Thanks Q! That was cute," she was smiling from ear to ear.

"Here you go sir. You get a teddy bear for winning three games in a row," said the old carnie as he handed Q a brown, fluffy teddy bear holding a black heart

"For you," Q said as he handed the prize over to Kim. Kim loved how smooth he was trying to be, but she was still thinking about his friend.

"So, you and Toya only friends for real? I know sometimes those be code words for other type of relationships," Kim laughed as she joked with Q but expected a truthful answer.

"If you're tryna find out if it's okay for you to fuck with me it is," Q smiled. "Yes, we're just best friends. She's my sister from another mister," Q joked confirming what Kim already thought.

"And who said I wanted to fuck with you? Please, don't flatter yourself," she told Q as she rolled her eyes.

"I can see it all in your eyes," Q looked directly at her when he said this. Kim was shy, but she was usually the flirter and the one to take charge when it came to men, but for some reason Q had her stuck.

Kim pulled her sunglasses out of her pocketbook, put them on and walked away from Q. She didn't like the feeling he was giving her. She had butterflies and she couldn't control it. Q laughed as he watched her walk away. *I'm gonna get her* he said to himself as he rubbed his hands together. They enjoyed the rest of their night and went home by the time Momma Margaret gave them.

Back home Kim went to sleep thinking about Q. She had never felt the way he made her feel that night and she wondered what it was. She went to sleep looking forward to the next day. Toya told her they would be hanging out with Q again.

All this thinking made her feel impatient. She didn't know if it was anxiety or paranoia, but she called Q again to see where he was. It rang twice then went to voicemail. She dialed his number again with shaky hands and it did the same thing. *Take a deep breath Kim, just breath bitch* she told herself trying to relax. *He's coming don't worry.* She knew Q wouldn't leave her stranded *but damn what was taking so long* she thought.

Seconds after this thought Q walked into the pizza spot like he owned it. She watched his eyes scatter around the place looking for her and when they locked eyes, she felt warm. She was so thankful for this man. Q saw it all in Kim's face, either hell was knocking at her door or on its way upstairs, he sensed her fear. He hugged her as soon as he got close enough. He didn't know what was going on, but he knew she needed it.

It took everything in Kim not to break down in Q's arms. She felt so safe next to him, but she told herself she was burying the pain and that's what she meant. She closed her eyes and enjoyed her hug.

CHAPTER THREE

So many thoughts were running through Kim's mind now that she was in the car with Q and she knew she had to figure something out fast. Just a few hours ago, she found their best friend's dead body and she knew it was only a matter of time before the news spread.

The police said they would be in her apartment for a while. They had to thoroughly search the place but by now Kim was sure that they had made their disturbing call to her family. Kim looked down at her cell phone and turned it off. She knew the main person that would be calling her phone was Toya's mom and she couldn't answer her right now about her daughter. *I'm sorry Momma Margaret* Kim whispered to herself. She knew how bad this was going to be for her.

Toya was a beautiful person outside of her line of work, and she was loved by so many. Kim looked over at Q and then looked down at his phone. She knew his would more than likely be ringing soon with the awful news.

"Let me see ya phone Q," Kim said like something was wrong.

"My phone is off. I didn't have any service in the tunnel, and I couldn't even call you while I was on my way to make sure you was aight. What the fuck is going on Kim? Like what is it? Talk to me!" Q was worried and angry now.

He had a soft spot for Kim, so her being in this state was starting to get to him. He just wanted to know what the problem was so he could fix it. There wasn't anything he wouldn't do for her.

He turned his phone back on now that Kim had mentioned it. He was probably missing business calls himself he thought. Kim knew this was it, if she didn't come out and tell him someone on the other side of his phone was going to once it was fully on.

"Yo Qazir, I don't even know how to tell you this shit," Kim had to stop and hold back tears.

"TELL ME WHAT KIM?! TELL ME FUCKING WHAT YO?!" Q yelled as he pulled over. He didn't like the vibe Kim was giving off and he knew something was wrong when she called him by his real name. He was done trying to figure shit out.

"It's Toya Q, she . . . she's gone."

. "What?" Q asked her calmly as if she said something stupid.

"I went to her crib today and she was dead," Kim couldn't believe her own words.

Q's phone started ringing off the hook, he had service now. It took a few rings for him to realize it was going off. He was still stuck on what Kim had just told him. He looked down at his phone screen and saw *Momma M* calling, that was Momma Margaret. He looked up at Kim and felt hot.

"What are you talking about Kim?" he asked calmly and stern.

"Toya's gone… somebody killed her in her apartment Q. I went over there like I always do, and she was dead. I sat there fucked up for a while, and then I called the cops. I stayed until they took her body out." Kim looked Q in the eyes as she told him this devastating news and she saw the pain all in them. Q's entire demeanor changed after hearing this. He looked as if his whole world just went bad. His eyes were sad and confused while trying not to water.

He turned away from Kim and put his head all the way back as if he was looking up into the sky for something. After a few seconds he lifted his head up and took a deep breath. The sound of the air leaving his mouth was loud and long. He didn't say anything. Kim didn't know what she should do. She'd never seen him like this before.

She put her hand on his shoulder and he didn't move or say a word. He pulled off and drove in silence. Kim decided to stay quiet and give him his time. She kept her hand on his shoulder.

"Oh-ooh Child" by The Five Stairsteps started playing on the radio. Kim got even more emotional, she shut the radio off. Q pulled over at the first place he could park and jumped out of the car. Kim watched him from the rearview mirror as he walked away with his hands on his head, looking up to the sky again. She knew her nigga was hurt.

Q stood frozen, looking up to the sky for what felt like forever but was actually a few minutes. He sat down on the dirty curb. He didn't give a damn how many pigeons done shitted on this sidewalk. Nothing mattered to him right now.

Not my fucking sister, Q said to himself. He thought about him and Toya's relationship. It was stronger than him and any of his friend's relationships, including Kim. Toya was his little sister, and even though they didn't share the same blood, it didn't make a difference.

Q started thinking about all the girls Toya used to beat up in the yard for him when they were little. She never let anybody bother him and vice versa. They protected each other. This made him think about the first time he met Toya.

It was a hot summer day and all the kids were playing in the yard. One of the boys from the neighborhood had unscrewed the fire hydrant and everyone was getting wet. Q and one of his homeboys had just come back from the corner store and they didn't want to play. Yes, it was hot, but they weren't in the mood to get messy with the water. They were both minding their business sitting on a bench when two girls from the yard walked over to them holding water balloons.

"What's up Q? You look hot," one of the girls giggled acting like she was going to throw the balloon at him.

"I ain't even playing Gloria, take that back over there." Q was serious when he said this but Gloria didn't want to hear it.

"Let me cool you down," Gloria kept playing with Q.

"I said I'm not…" before Q could finish his sentence, Gloria threw a balloon directly in his face and it popped, wetting him all over. Gloria took off running as if it was funny. Q was vexed!

"This dumb bitch thinks I'm a joke?" Q got up to go after Gloria. She just disrespected him, and even as a youngin' he took his respect seriously, from both females and males.

"This bitch is so lucky I ain't got sisters man!" Q said to his homeboy.

"Forget her bro. She just plays too much," Q's friend said trying to get his mind off of what just happened.

He knew it wasn't going to work. Gloria should have never thrown that balloon at him. He knew his friend was pissed and was probably going to hit a female, making the situation worse.

Toya was watching the whole incident from the slide. She couldn't stand Gloria. She was one of the older, fast girls in the yard. She developed quicker than others and she let it go to her head. She always thought she could say and do whatever to the boys because she was cute with big boobs.

Wrong nigga bitch. Toya thought to herself. She was glad Q was after this chick, she couldn't wait for one of the guys to embarrass her. Most of them fell for her big boobs or her face, and let her get away with murder but Toya saw that Q wasn't impressed. She followed behind him and his friend as they walked after Gloria. She wanted to have front row seats for Gloria's embarrassment.

"Didn't I tell you I wasn't fucking playing?" Q was almost in Gloria's face.

"Damn yo, you that scared of water? I was just playing" Gloria said with no respect or apology. Q wanted to hit her so bad, "I don't give a fuck! I told you I wasn't playing! You're so lucky I don't hit girls," he said with base in his voice.

"Yeah, yeah. You scared of water bruh, like I said," Gloria was still rude and had no type of remorse for what she did.

She was still disrespecting Q. Toya was watching from the side pissed off. She couldn't believe Q wasn't going to at least slap her. *It's good he didn't hit females but then what about when these hoes get out of line?* Toya thought. Q couldn't believe that she was still so disrespectful.

"Yo, I got $100 for whoever beats this bitch up," he was serious as he yelled this out to the other girls in the yard. Gloria started laughing like he was a joke.

"Yeah, right boy, please!" Gloria said waving her hand, ready to walk away. Toya did not waste any more time hoping and wishing Q had hit her. She jumped in front of Gloria as she tried to walk away and asked her for her head up. Gloria thought Toya was a joke; she didn't take her serious.

"Girl, bye," she said as she laughed in Toya's face and tried to walk away again. She made a mistake thinking Toya was playing. Toya followed behind her and whooped her ass in the yard in front of Q with everyone else watching. She didn't really want the money. She did it because she knew Gloria needed to learn a lesson. *Now what if Q did have a sister?* Toya thought, *all that shit you poppin' to him and you can't even fight.* Toya watched as Gloria got up embarrassed and ran off. That was the last time her or any of the girls in the yard fucked with Q.

"Yo! You whipped home girl's ass! I gotta give you $200!" Q said excitedly.

"I ain't do it for the money. She needed to learn a lesson and I respect that you don't hit girls. I don't know what you gonna do the next time one of these hoes get outta line tho," Toya was speaking almost as if she was a homeboy. Q liked her.

"Imma call you lil sis from now on," Q joked and laughed. Toya didn't crack a smile or laugh.

"Nah, all jokes aside I appreciate that, and I got ya back if any of these fuck niggas ever try you and that's my word!" Q let Toya know he was serious. "What's ya name anyway?" he asked.

"Toya, and so what we supposed to be power rangers defending each other now?" Toya laughed at her own joke and so did Q.

"Well Toya, imma call you T, and I'm deadass, if *anybody* fucks with you, you let me know. You gone be my sister from another mister," he joked but seriously meant it.

"And who you supposed to be around here?" Toya asked with a smile.

"I'm Q baby. I'm gonna take over soon," he looked at Toya and meant his words.

"Aight, aight, I hear that. Pound it," Toya told Q putting her fist out for him to tap her fist with his.

"Pound it!" Q said putting his fist out and laughing. From that day been on they were inseparable.

Q felt like he failed Toya for letting this happen. He was confused. This was his town. He stayed low key but he made all the moves. He knew about everything going on in this neighborhood. *How the fuck did someone merk Toya? Who the fuck would even want to hurt her?* Q was questioning himself. She had a bunch of hating ass females that didn't like her but it wasn't that serious and Q didn't think this was a female's job. He couldn't figure the shit out and it was hurting him even more.

He thought about Kim as he looked over at the car, *did she know something and wasn't telling me,* he thought. *Nah, Kim tells me everything,* he said to himself, so he thought. He knew how hard this had to be for Kim, her and Toya were *Thelma and Louise* to him. He would even get playfully jealous sometimes at how tight they were. Toya always joked on how that's why he always wanted to get with Kim. He wanted to get with Kim because she was dope, he couldn't resist her vibe. Even now as friends, after their relationship didn't work out, he still felt the same and no matter what. That was his bitch.

Q couldn't remember the last time he cried. He was a man, he was a thug, but he had a heart. Toya's death hurt him to the core. He knew he had to figure out who did this and kill them. He couldn't let this slide at all. It was war time. He was going to find out whom, when, and why, if it was the last thing he did. He got up, wiped the tears off his face, and got back into the car.

He was quiet for the rest of the drive to his house. Not a word was said. He thought about all of the times that he had shared with Toya from the age of seven until yesterday. He was lost and confused and he needed answers.

Kim watched Q drive in silence and she knew he wasn't the same man he was about an hour ago. This fucked with him the same way it did with her if not more. Toya and Q's relationship was different; their brother-sister bond was something serious. Blood couldn't make them any closer. There was no way that Kim could tell him what they were into. She sat back and tried to gather her thoughts for the rest of the ride. She looked over at Q and could tell he was thinking about something vicious. She didn't know exactly what but she would almost bet her life that it had to do with finding the people responsible. She knew she had to figure something out, and figure it out fast.

CHAPTER FOUR

When they finally pulled up to Q's spot, there was still silence. You could almost hear the pain in the air. Kim looked around Q's apartment. It was nice and neat like always. She could tell that there was no woman's touch but between Q and his butler, it stayed tidy. In his living room he had pictures up of him and his mom, him and Toya, and him and Momma Margaret. Kim loved the way Q honored his family, he would do anything for them and his love for them always showed.

Kim stared at the picture of him and Toya. It looked like they were in the yard and they both had bright smiles on their faces while hugging each other. She immediately felt guilt in her soul. She knew Toya's death had to be killing Q inside and she didn't have the heart to tell him the truth. She didn't know if it was a good idea to bother Q or not but she hated seeing him like this.

The awkward silence between them was bothering Kim now so she decided to break it. "Q, you're scaring me now. Could you please talk to me?" Kim tried. Q hadn't said a word to her since she told him about Toya and it had been well over an hour. He completely ignored Kim as if he didn't hear or see her at all. She walked up to him and put her hands on both of his shoulders, standing directly in front of him.

"Q, I know it's fucked up baby, I know," Kim said as she hugged him softly. Kim's hug seemed to be all Q needed. He gave in after that and cried like a baby. He cried as if no one was there.

"T was my fucking heart yo," Q said with hurt in his voice. Kim couldn't fight her tears back this time. She knew she had promised herself that she wouldn't get into her emotions but she couldn't control it. She cried with Q and Q cried with her. They were both missing the same piece of their hearts. Kim cried with pain, hurt, and guilt. She knew she should've been dead with her friend.

After they let their tears out with each other, they both seemed a little better. They were talking now and the apartment didn't seem so empty. Kim felt drained. "I need to lay down," she told Q while holding her head. She needed sleep. It'd been a long day, and she knew her days coming were only going to be longer. She looked at her phone still powered off and thought about all the stress it would bring if she was to turn it on. She decided to keep it off, at least until the morning. She took her clothes off and walked over to Q's bed where he was sitting.

"Can I lay down?" she asked him. Q looked Kim's naked body up and down like it was the first time he'd seen her this way. He thought about how much he used to dick her down. Their sex life was one of the best parts of their relationship and they vowed to never cross that line again once they became friends.

"Yeah babe, come on," he said as he grabbed her by the waist and pulled her onto the bed. He removed his clothes and laid down next to her. He pulled her closer to him and wrapped his arms around her naked body and soft skin. It'd been a long while since he'd cuddled with Kim and it was fucking with his mind for three different reasons. One, was the fact that he wouldn't be able to tell Toya tomorrow. Two, was because Toya was what brought them here. And three, was the fact that he didn't know what happened. It made no sense, and the next, closest person to Toya was Kim, and she didn't know either.

He looked down at Kim laying in his arms. She fell right asleep. He watched her sleeping body slowly move up and down with each breath she took. He knew he could trust her with his life and he felt guilty for questioning it, but something just wasn't right. He couldn't think of at least one reason why Kim would want to keep something about Toya's death a secret, but he felt like if anybody would have known, it would be her. He took a deep breath as he felt bad about his thoughts. He pushed all of these speculations out of his head and cuddled Kim tighter. It was just them now, he thought. He closed his eyes and drifted off to sleep.

Kim suddenly opened her eyes. She woke up and couldn't go back to sleep at all. She was laying in Q's arms with mixed emotions and feelings. At this point she knew he was her last source of life. He could protect her, he could help her, and most of all he would want to get the bastards who killed Toya. *But was she ready to bring Q to that side of her world?* she thought and asked herself. Her and Toya were into some crazy shit and it had become dangerous. They were ready to leave that life alone and move on right before Toya was killed. She knew the consequences of their actions, but she thought somehow, they were smart enough to get out alive.

Kim rolled over and was facing Q now, watching him sleep. *Can I tell you this secret? Would you still respect me?* She asked him questions in her own head. The only way to find out was to just tell him. She took a deep breath and wiped her thumb over his right eyebrow. They were so thick, and a few hairs were out of place.

She thought about the first time she ever gave herself to Q. It was about two weeks after they made it official at the block party. Toya and Kim were hanging out on their stoop smoking and chillin' as usual. Kim caught a text from Q saying *roll up*. She knew this meant he wanted to see her. Q wasn't a smoker, he would only drink. He knew Kim loved to get high so he would let her roll up and listen to her high thoughts. She smiled as she texted him back, *come get me*.

"I'm about to go see Q girl," Kim told Toya.

"Whaaaat?" Toya said with a Kool-Aid smile.

"Yes, girl. You know Q is my man. We just having fun right now."

Kim got up and got ready for Q to pick her up. She wanted to be nice and fresh. She had plans for things to go all the way. Toya was still sitting outside on the stoop while Kim was inside changing. Q pulled up beeping his horn.

"Y'all better behave y'all selves," Toya yelled to Q.

"I'm always well-behaved sis you know that," Q laughed as he answered Toya.

Kim came running to the door screaming out for Q to hold on.

"You know how she always drags it bro," Toya joked to Q.

"I know, we ain't going nowhere *fancy*," Q laughed. After about five minutes of waiting for Kim, Toya got up and walked over to Q's car. She knew it would have taken her friend about 10 more minutes to come out.

"So, where y'all going?" Toya asked as she sat in the car.

"Daaaamn nosey!" Q joked. He was always able to be his playful self around Toya. "Nah, I'm boutta take her to the telly and blow her back out. You know me," Q spoke cockily but was joking.

"Nigga, shut the fuck up!" Toya laughed hard. "You ain't blowing shit out."

Q became serious, "Nah let me stop, we ain't going nowhere we about to just chill and hang out, you know? Don't worry, I'll bring your friend back soon," Q teased Toya.

"She was my damn friend first, remember that!" Toya joked back with Q.

Kim came running outside now ready to jump in the car. Toya got out and told them to have fun. "We will," Kim said waving goodbye to her friend.

"So, where we going?" Kim asked Q excitedly as soon as she got into the car. She was ready to take things to another level as soon as she got alone with him. He made it clear at the party that he wanted her, so she was going to make the first move.

"Just sit back, relax and enjoy the ride baby girl," he told her as he rolled the windows down and turned the music up. Kim smiled at how smooth Q used to think he was. Watching him sleep now, she wanted to kiss all over his face. She continued to remember their time together.

Q pulled up to a hotel that was about forty five minutes away from them. They checked into a suite with a huge hot tub. Kim knew right away they were going to have some fun. "You should've told me to bring my bathing suit," Kim flirted with Q as she walked around the room checking it out. "Your birthday suit will do just fine," Q flirted back.

Kim smiled. She liked the fact that Q already had sex on his mind. She was ready to take their relationship to the next level. She wasted no time and walked over to the hot tub taking her clothes off. She left on her bra and panties as she turned the water on. She walked back over to Q and put her hands on his face. She looked him in the eyes and then gave him a long passionate deep kiss. She kissed Q with no problem. Even though she hated kissing men, she felt like Q was different. Q enjoyed Kim's kiss as he held the back of her head and kissed her back harder. They occupied the same spot, kissing for a few minutes.

Kim stepped back and looked at Q. His fine black skin was shining as always and his angelic smile made him even more desirable. She pulled his shirt over his head and admired his chocolate chest. She rubbed her hands all over his muscles and his six pack. She kissed him from his neck to his chest, slowly and passionately. Q watched as Kim took control. He loved how she always wanted to be in charge. He was going to allow her to be dominant until he was ready to show her who was really boss. She was down on her knees now ready to pull his dick out. Q smiled as he watched her snatch his dick out from his pants and put it in her mouth. It turned him on more knowing she wanted to do it for her own pleasure.

He let her play around a little bit before taking control. He grabbed her mouth and her cheeks and tapped his dick on her lips. He rubbed the tip of his dick around the inside of her mouth while tapping it on her tongue.

"You wanna suck on daddy's dick?" Q asked Kim in a low but rough tone as spit rolled off her lips.

"Mmm…I wanna suck on daddy's dick until it cums," Kim answered in a seductive baby voice licking the spit from falling off her lips.

"Oh yeah? So, come make daddy cum," Q sat down on the couch now while Kim was on her knees in front of him. She sucked his dick like she saw the girls do on the porno movies she would sneak and watch at night. She closed her eyes as she copied their techniques.

She slurped, sucked and choked on his dick while he moaned.

The sound of Q's voice made Kim's pussy wetter than it already was. She started touching on herself while still sucking on his penis. Q heard Kim's moan causing him to look up, he saw her touching her pussy and he wanted to ram his dick inside of her right then and there. He watched her as she sucked on him like an ice pop and rubbed on her clit while her eyes rolled to the back of her head.

He couldn't resist anymore so he stopped her from sucking and threw her on her back. He spread her legs wide open and kissed the inside of her thighs until he reached her pussy. He licked her clit up and down with his wide, wet tongue. Kim let out a loud gasp as she opened her legs wider. She wanted Q to have all access to her womanhood. He kissed her pussy as she moved her hips up and down. Q was teasing her and she was becoming anxious.

"You want daddy to suck on it?" Q asked her seductively.

"Yes," Kim screamed out horny as ever. "Say please," Q smiled as he watched Kim's facial expression turn into that of a begging child.

"Can you suck on it pleaseee?" Kim dragged her words. Q began sucking on Kim's pussy like it was peach cobbler on a Sunday. He licked, sucked, bit, and made a mess on his face as he pleased his woman. Kim came multiple times back-to-back while Q continued to eat her and swallow her juices at the same time. She looked down at him and loved the way his beard looked with her juices dripping from it, she could tell that she tasted good to him.

"Put it in me please," Kim cried out, she couldn't take anymore her body was throbbing and she wanted to feel Q inside of her. Q stopped sucking on her clit and kissed it one last time. He grabbed his dick and tapped on Kim's pussy with the tip of it. Kim moved her hips in a circular motion letting Q know she was ready for him to enter her. He slid himself in and was caught off guard at how tight she was. He heard Kim gasp for air as he tried to push himself harder inside of her. He looked down at her and saw her face scrunched up.

"Kim, I know you ain't no virgin," Q stopped trying to force himself inside of her. Kim was embarrassed. She always watched porn movies and she flirted with guys as if she was experienced. She thought since she studied these videos so well, she would be ready when the time came.

"Yeah, I am," she confirmed Q's thoughts as she looked down ashamed.

"Damn girl you sure don't seem like no motherfucking virgin," Q was serious. Kim talked as if she was a pro in bed before they took it this far and her head game, which Q had just received definitely seemed experienced.

"Yo you sure you wanna do this with me? I don't really know if I'm the type of nigga to be taking virginities and shit," Q joked, but he was serious. He was older than Kim and he knew her innocence was everything she had. He loved her and he cared about her but he didn't know if he deserved to be her first. "I'm here ain't I?" Kim asked Q. "Don't I seem ready the way

I just sucked your dick, I'm a big girl Q, I know what I want. I want you and I want you to have me. So, come on and bust my cherry."

Kim meant what she said and she was determined, Q smiled. He loved the fact that she knew what she wanted and she was so real about it. He knew after this Kim was going to most definitely be his bitch. He slid inside of her gently and slowly taking it easy this time. He grew harder with each stroke as Kim's tight pussy gripped his dick.

After minutes, her pain turned into pleasure as he opened her up more and more with each stroke. He made sure to go slow so he wouldn't rip her hymen too much. This was the first time he had ever taken anyone's virginity.

Kim was enjoying every moment of it. She would often dream what sex would be like and she knew once she got past the first time she would enjoy it. She knew she wanted Q to take her virginity after he revealed his feelings for her at the block party. He was the only guy that gave her a right kind of feeling.

After their first round of sex Kim was completely open and she wanted him more. Her and Q fucked all night, everywhere in the room. From the dressers to the shower, they blessed every space with their sexual energy. They fell asleep naked in each other's arms feeling amazed.

Kim came back to her senses, shaking these memories out of her head. Her thoughts came back to reality and she decided she'd tell Q everything after

Toya's funeral. She kissed him on his lips, turned around and tried to get some more sleep.

Q woke up sweating. He turned and looked at the alarm clock on his night stand, it was 3:52 a.m. He couldn't go back to sleep. He thought about Toya and felt cold. *Why T?* He thought to himself, *who could want to hurt you?* He looked over at Kim while she was asleep. *What's really going on KP?* He was questioning her again. *You can tell me anything. You usually tell me everything, why can't you tell me something?*

He had so many questions he wanted to ask her. He put his hands on his head with mixed feelings. Here he was again, questioning Kim's loyalty. *But why? Was he wrong? Or was he on to something?* His thoughts were all over the place. Him and Toya had a bond that was out of this world. *Was Toya tryna tell him something?* Q started feeling a little crazy. *Let me chill out,* he told himself as he shook the thoughts out of his head once again. He rolled over and tried to force himself back to sleep.

The next morning Kim woke up sick, she ran to the bathroom to vomit as her stomach curled up. She knew it was between the baby and her not being able to eat at all. She spent about ten minutes over the toilet, throwing her insides up every few seconds before she could get up and get herself together. She walked back into the room and saw that Q was up and gone. She looked over at the clock, thinking it was still early but when she saw 12:23 p.m., she knew she had just overslept. The rest was well needed so she didn't mind.

She looked in Q's closet and grabbed an extra towel and washcloth. She turned the TV on so it wouldn't be so quiet. *"Breaking News; On East 94th Street a twenty...,"* Kim turned the TV right off. She knew they were going to be talking about Toya and she didn't want to hear anything about it right then. She turned the radio on instead and let the music play. She turned it up loud so she could hear it over the water. She finally walked into the bathroom to get in the splash, it was long overdue. She turned the water on and tied her long thick hair into a bun.

She took her time in the shower, thinking and reflecting on everything that was going on in her life. She allowed the steaming hot water to run over her body from head to toe and it relaxed her. Memories of her and Toya kept playing over and over in her head; she just couldn't take her mind off of her. She started to feel how she felt the first time she found Toya's dead body. She was breathing heavy and her body was anxious, *was every day going to be like this,* she wondered to herself. She thought she was stronger than this but this pain was much heavier for her to carry. In her heart, she knew exactly why she was feeling the way she felt. She took a deep breath, calming herself down and began to wash up.

"Though I'm missing you, (Although Im missing you), I'll find a way to get through, (I'll find a way to get through), living without you Cause you were my sister, my strength, and my pride only god may know why, still I will get by..."

"Missing You" by Brandy, Gladys Knight, Tamia, and Chaka Khan was playing on the radio and Kim refused to leave the shower to turn it off. She was weak, she was worn out, and the words from the speaker were touching her soul. Not to mention the song was from one of Toya's favorite movies, *Set It Off.* Kim was sick to her soul. If she was crying, she couldn't tell because the water was washing all of her tears away.

Now that you're gone, every day I go on, (I go on) but life's just not the same (life's just not the same). I'm so empty inside and my tears I can't hide but I'll try I'll try to face the pain.

Kim cried and cried as the song played through the speakers. She cried until she couldn't cry anymore. *Was Toya trying to tell her something?* Kim started to think to herself. This made it harder for her to stop crying. *I miss you too T, I miss you too so much please save a spot for me.* Kim blew a kiss up to the sky with tears in her eyes. Her tears turned to anger. Revenge was the only feeling she felt. She knew today, she had no choice but to put her big girl panties on and face reality. Toya was dead, her family was going to want answers, and she had a funeral that she had to help plan. She took a long deep breath thinking of all of this. She knew she had to do what she had to do.

Q had barely slept when his phone started going off at 7 a.m. He looked and saw it was Momma Margaret calling. He started to feel uneasy. He had no thoughts of what he was going to say to her that could make anything better. He knew if this had broken anyone's heart, this broke Momma Margaret's the most. Toya was her pride and joy and her only daughter.

"Hi ma, how are you doing this morning?" he asked as he answered the phone, knowing her morning was probably horrible and her night was even worse. Momma Margaret was sniffling, and Q could tell she was still crying.

"My baby is gone Q! Did you know that? Did you know that somebody killed my baby? MY BABY! Not a random person but my goddamn baby, our Toya!" Momma Margaret said, hysterically crying on her end of the phone. "Q, who could have done this? WHO!?" She asked angrily. Q heard it all in her voice. He felt responsible again for letting this happen.

"Ma, I love you and I've been fucked up since I heard this shit. I don't know what to say, think, or do," Q said honestly. He looked over at Kim sleeping. It was a long quiet pause on the phone before he spoke again. "I'll be over in a little bit Ma, see you soon."

Q hung up the phone as he turned to look back at Kim. The pressure was building up now that Momma wanted answers just as much as he did. He wondered to himself if he should speak to Momma about his suspicions of Kim. He ruled against it as he thought about how much it would upset her and he wasn't completely sure that what he thought was true. He rolled over and slowly got up out of the bed, trying not to wake

Kim. He grabbed a towel and went to the bathroom. He took a nice, long, hot shower, got dressed and headed out the door to visit Momma Margaret as he had promised.

After Kim showered, she found an old pair of sweatpants that belonged to Q and threw on one of his T-shirts. She didn't even care how she looked. She felt comfortable. She headed out the door to go see Momma Margaret. She knew this was going to be hard.

CHAPTER FIVE

Kim took the subway to see Momma Margaret. It reminded her of the good old days when they all used to take the subway together. Momma Margaret was like a mother to all of Toya's friends, especially Q. He was like the son she never had, and she always told him this. Kim smiled, everybody loved Q and you couldn't blame them.

When Kim reached Momma Margaret's place, she saw Q's car outside. It made her feel a little at ease knowing she wouldn't be alone. She was afraid to see what condition Momma Margaret was in. She could only imagine how hard this had to be for her.

When Kim walked inside, she instantly felt the difference in Momma's house. She felt something missing. It didn't feel the same as it did when Toya was here, and she felt it as she looked around.

There was no fresh air flowing through the house, there was nothing brewing on the stove, not even hot water for coffee, it felt empty. As she continued to walk inside, she could finally hear some life. It sounded like music coming from Momma's room in the back. She walked a little quicker now to get away from the emptiness she felt around her.

When she walked in Momma's room there was a video playing on the TV of Toya at what seemed to be her 5th birthday party. She was dressed as a beautiful princess in a white ball gown. Momma Margaret always kept and cherished things like these. Toya was singing and dancing in the video while twirling around in her princess dress. It was like watching an angel on the big screen. This brought a little tear to Kim's eye but she held it together.

When Momma saw Kim, she smiled. "Hi baby," she said, reaching her arms out to give Kim a hug.

"Hi Momma, how are you? I'm sorry it took so long for me to get here," she said as she gave Momma a tight hug.

"It's ok baby, its ok," Momma said hugging Kim back tighter and rubbing her back. It seemed like they both needed this hug.

Q got up and also gave Momma a hug with a kiss on her forehead, "I'll be back. I'm gonna go check on the flower arrangements. Kim, call me when you leave Momma's." He walked out of the room leaving them alone.

It was just Momma Margaret, Kim, and baby Toya on the screen now. They sat in silence watching. Every few seconds you could hear Momma's sniffles and could tell she was weeping.

"Momma, I don't even know what to say. I can't even believe this myself. I can't imagine how you feel," Kim said rubbing Mommas arm.

Momma Margaret placed her hand on Kim's hand as she was rubbing, "Toya was my baby girl, she was special. I feel like I lost my light inside, baby I feel like my soul is gone. What I can't imagine is how I'm going to live the rest of my days without her. I thought I was gonna see my baby get married. I thought I was gonna have me some grandbabies. What happens now? I plan a funeral? I put my baby in the ground? And that's it? I come home to an empty house? A million memories of Toya but no Toya? Toya's clothes...but no Toya? Toya's Momma...but no Toya," Momma Margaret broke down crying hysterically. Kim just rubbed her back and cried with her. She didn't offer any words she just listened and cried with her.

"I need my child back! I need my child baaaaack! I need my damn child baaaaaaack!" Momma Margaret was screaming with anger now. She was rocking back and forth just screaming and crying. "Do you know, my baby just came to me yesterday and she said, Momma I'm about to be a grown woman now. I said child please, you gone always be my baby. She said no Momma, for real. I'm about to go live my life for real. I just wanted to tell you how much I love and appreciate you, and I want you to always know, no matter where I go I will always be one call away."

Momma cried harder now as she repeated these words. Kim knew she was referring to Toya coming to say goodbye before they fled town.

"What were you into Toya? Who would wanna kill you? What is going on?" Momma asked the air as she continued to rock back and forth crying. "These sorry ass detectives can't tell me shit," Momma said angrily.

Kim sat in silence while Momma vented, and tears streamed down her face. She had the answers to all of Momma's questions. She had the answers to all of the detective's questions, she just couldn't say. Her and Toya had been into some foul shit, things went wrong and it ended up costing Toya her life. Kim knew that she could easily be next, she should be next, and she was lucky to still be alive. She kept rubbing Mommas back while she let her cries out.

Momma Margaret must've cried for hours and Kim stayed right by her side. She was missing her sister bad. It seemed like the more time that went by the more real it became. She knew that nothing was gonna be the same anymore.

After her cries were all out, Momma started asking Kim for suggestions for the funeral. They picked out which pictures to use and where the flowers would go. Together they decided everyone would wear yellow and white, and her immediate family would wear all white. Yellow was Toya's favorite color and it felt warm.

The last thing Momma Margaret had to do was pick out an outfit for Toya to wear and a casket for her to rest eternally in. This was the hardest thing she had ever had to do. Kim told Momma she'd do it and she'd make sure it was beautiful. Momma wanted a fast funeral. She wanted to get it done and over with. There was no joy in anything she had to do, so she felt that there was no reason to drag the process on. The funeral would be held in two days and it would be one service, then straight to burial.

Kim needed the time she spent with Momma. She could tell Momma needed it and she was gonna need a lot more throughout this nightmare. There was no doubt in the world that Kim loved Toya and no doubt in the universe that if she had been there that day, they would be dead together and they would've gone out with a bang.

Kim realized that she couldn't keep beating herself up and blaming herself for Toya's death. Neither one of them wanted this but they both knew when they got involved what came with it. Now that Toya was gone all Kim could really do is live life with the memories that they shared, after she found and killed the people responsible.

"Alright Momma imma go check on Q and get some rest. Are you going to be alright in here alone?" Kim asked as she stood up to get ready to leave.

"Baby, I'm never alone with Jesus by my side," Momma Margaret replied. Kim smiled, she admired the strength Momma carried. "I will be just fine. Now you promise me you gone check on Q. He's not taking this too well and I can tell it changed him inside just as much as it changed me. I can see it in his eyes that he's going to do something vicious. Now I want these bastards just as dead as he does, but I don't wanna lose another child. Tell him I said to move smart and be safe."

Momma gave Kim a hug. Kim understood Momma's promise that she wanted her to make. Momma knew Q was going to kill somebody. She did not condone violence in any way whatsoever, but someone had killed her only daughter. She wanted him to handle it, but she wanted him to be safe while doing it.

Kim felt the same way. She wished that she could just tell Momma the truth and tell her she was going to make sure she caught the people responsible for their heartache, but she couldn't.

"I'll make sure he knows how you feel Momma, believe me," Kim reassured her. Momma turned around to open her front door and Detectives White and Dawson were standing there ready to knock. Kim looked over at Momma and rolled her eyes when she saw them. She wasn't expecting them to be there.

"Hello Mrs. Richards. How are you today? I'm sorry to bother you, but I was wondering if you'd mind answering just a few more questions for me please," Detective White asked with her notepad in her hand.

"Do you know who murdered my child Detective White?" Momma asked with misery in her voice.

"I'm deeply sorry Mrs. Richards, we do not at this time, but that's why we're here, see I was..." Detective White's statement was cut short when Momma interrupted her.

"Then get the hell off of my porch," Momma said as she slammed her door in the detectives faces. Kim looked at her and smiled. She knew Momma would be able to handle herself while her and Q got to the bottom of things. Q popped in her head. She had to stick to her word and tell him after the funeral.

After a few minutes Kim walked outside and spotted the detectives parked on the corner. Before she could turn and walk the other way, they saw her and started their engine up. *Now these motherfuckers are gonna stalk me* she thought to herself as she walked faster. The subway was just down the block, not too far away. Kim thought she could make it and avoid them.

"Are you in a hurry Ms. Carter?" Detective White asked Kim through her passenger side window as detective Dawson drove along side of her.

"Yes, as a matter of fact I am," She answered the detective in a snobby tone. She wasn't going to pretend to be nice anymore. She didn't want anything to do with them and she wanted it to be known.

"Well, I was wondering if I could ask you a few more questions about Ms. Richards," the detective said in a persistent tone.

"Didn't you hear her Momma back there? You're asking us all these damn questions like we supposed to help you catch the person that did it. That's *YOUR* job and I'm sure there are more people who you could be harassing, and who could give you real information." Kim was almost yelling at the detective now.

"Stop the car!" Detective White ordered to her partner. She got out of the car and walked over to Kim, standing in front of her now. "Now listen to me Ms. Carter, I am trying to find the lowlifes who did this to your friend. I have no leads, no witnesses, no evidence…

nothing. If you wanted these animals behind bars the way you say you do, then you should be glad to help me figure some shit out. Now we found some money in Ms. Richard's apartment, a lot of money without anything to account for it. Now, I don't know, maybe she was into some bad things and she got caught up with the wrong people. Usually when we see cases like this, it turns out that there are some type of *illegal* activities going on. Now again, are you sure that there's *nothing* you may know about your friend's murder that can possibly help us?" Detective White looked Kim directly in her eyes with a serious snare.

"Wow," Kim looked the detective back into her eyes and looked surprised. "So now, because you can't do *your* job correctly and find the murderer, you're going to discriminate against my friend over some money *you* snooped and found? I guess because she was young, *African American*, and in the hood, she couldn't have a lousy ass 10 stacks saved in her home? So, because she was black with money saved up, not put in these cracker ass banks that can do whatever with your money, she has to be into some type of *illegal* business? Listen, I'm going to make sure the whole *fuckin'* precinct knows about your accusations Detective *White*. I knew everything about my goddamn friend, and she wasn't into shit illegal. If you *must* know, we use to strip, I know you know a bunch of young black girls in that field, don't you Detective White? Toya was saving that *money* up to open her own business one day. She had dreams and goals just like the little *white* girls whose cases y'all solve in a week. I'd appreciate it if you'd let my friend's name rest in peace without these *nasty* rumors you're trying to brew up. Don't come back around here until you have a name. Now you have a great day detective…"

Kim felt great after telling the detective off. She knew inside that she was lying but she didn't care. She knew that detective didn't know anything, and she knew she surely didn't know enough to accuse Toya. Kim walked off and went into the subway leaving Detective White standing on the corner by herself, dissatisfied.

"God dammit White! I told you!" Detective Dawson said in the driver seat, upset and ready to pull off. "Now if she calls the Chief and reports this that's your ass not mine!" Detective Dawson yelled.

"Dammit Dave, I really wish you would calm the hell down!" Detective White yelled back. "Look, she's not going to report shit," Detective White said trying to reassure him.

"Oh yeah? And how exactly do you know that Julia?" he asked sarcastically.

"Because, she knows I'm right. I don't care what you say Dave, she knows I'm right. I didn't even tell her how much money we found, and she said $10,000," Detective White said as she wrote in her notepad.

"She knows everything about that damn girl. Don't you think she'd know how much money she had?" Dave asked Detective White with sarcasm still in his voice.

"Exactly my point Dave, she knows EVERYTHING," she answered.

Detective White jotted this down in her notepad and then closed it. She looked out the window as her partner continued to drive. *I'm going to get her* she thought to herself.

Kim rode the subway back to Q's with anxiety in her body. Everything was happening too fast for her. *Why didn't I take her money?* Kim thought to herself. While she was in Toya's apartment before the cops came, it never dawned on her to check for her money. She knew the detectives didn't find it all because they packed the money up they planned to leave with. The money the detectives found was the money Toya planned on giving to Momma Margaret. She still had it because she couldn't figure out a way to get Momma to accept it without thinking it was *dirty money*, as she would say. *Now Momma would never see it,* Kim thought, *there's no telling what those pigs would do with it.*

Kim knew she had to do something and do something fast. The detectives were too hot on her tail now. She was going to stick to her plan and tell Q everything after the funeral. She would need to get low *real* soon.

CHAPTER SIX

Back at home now Q was sick. After his visit with Momma Margaret, he felt like less of a man. How did he let this happen in his own hometown? Watching her cry the way she did felt the same to him as if he was watching the woman who birthed him cry. Blood wouldn't have made a difference, and it hurt his heart to witness it.

His mind went back to Kim. He didn't give a fuck about feeling guilty anymore. He needed answers and he wanted them yesterday. He decided that as soon as she got back, he would ask her if she knew anything. He had to get to the bottom of this and fast. Q's mind was racing when his phone started ringing.

"Yo," he answered. "I know you said don't call you until the job is complete boss, but it hasn't been easy. We're dealing with females and they tend to be sneakier," the voice on the other end of the phone said.

Q cut him off, "Wait, you said females?" Q asked shocked. "Yes, boss two of them. I got one out of here the other day and the other one I can't seem to locate yet. I was going to hold off until the funeral, but I just wanted to give you an update. I just got the pictures downloaded and printed out so now I have a better idea of who I'm looking for," the voice said nonchalantly, not knowing he just touched Q's soul with his information.

"Send me the pictures right now," Q said in a calm deep tone and then hung up the phone.

Q couldn't believe what he had just heard. His hands were shaking while waiting for the text from his hit man Frankie. As soon as his text went off, he downloaded the attachment and he couldn't believe his eyes.

There it was, a picture of Toya & Kim in colorful wigs and awful makeup. They tried to disguise themselves, but Q could spot his sister and his bitch from anywhere. He immediately called his hitta back.

"Yeah boss?" he answered on the first ring.

"Who took care of that first situation?" Q asked.

"Rico did boss. Why what's up? What you need?" he asked anxious ready to make a move.

"I need you and Rico to come to the office *NOW!*" Q said and hung up. His office wasn't far from where he lived at all, so he decided to walk, he needed some fresh air anyway.

Q couldn't fucking believe this shit. He knew his gut wasn't steering him wrong. He put a hit out on his own sister.

"WHAT THE FUCK T!" Q screamed out in the middle of the street like he was losing his mind. "What the fuck were y'all bitches thinking?" he asked himself out loud. About a month ago some of Q's men from out of town started getting hit up.

See, Q was a big-time drug pusher, who kept his line of work on the low. When he turned 18, he inherited money from his deceased father. His mother was young and single when she had him, but his father was older, and his name was attached to benefits. This was his front to people when he brought his first BMW after turning 18. He knew the money would not last him forever, so he invested most of it into drugs and business.

If his mother did anything right in her young scandalous life, she made sure Q started his adult life with something after she passed away when Q was only 17. He often thinks that his mother would be proud of the way he spent his inheritance.

All of his dirty work was done out of town and very rarely did his workers meet his family. It depended on their job title. Q moved smart with his operation, he opened places out of town and donated to almost all of the black charities in Brooklyn anonymously. He didn't open up any businesses in Brooklyn to keep from drawing attention, but he gave back to his community through their charities. He wasn't fly and flashy, but his demeanor demanded respect and recognition. He had a very well run organization going, and things moved smoothly.

What confused Q was who robbed him and why. He always kept his operations on the hush and away from his hometown. He liked being the man in silence. He didn't have any major enemies and he wasn't moving sloppy enough for outside niggas to hate and want to rob him. What confused him even more about the robberies that had recently taken place was the fact that they never left a trace and they never left a witness; they were cold blooded murderers.

It wasn't until the last robbery that Q was able to get a drop on the thieves. The situation must have gone wrong and they slipped up and made mistakes. They left a witness and a shitty video surveillance tape. Never once since this shit started did Q think it was females taking his cash and murking his men. And never once in a million years would he have ever thought it would be

Toya and Kim. This shit did not make any sense to him at all.

Were they hittin' his spots on purpose? Did they know about his business all this time? Q started questioning himself while walking. He was standing in the middle of the sidewalk, talking to himself, looking crazy.

"Nah, nah T wouldn't do that," Q said out loud.

They had to think it was somebody else's business he thought to himself *but how the hell would they even know about this?*

Suddenly it hit Q and he felt stupid. He had a snake in his front yard. This was the only idea that made any sense to Q but, who was the snake? He kept a solid gang, he came up with his same friends from the sandbox, and he never once questioned their loyalty. Q was stuck. The only men around him that came along during his come up were two of his hitmen, Frankie & Rico.

He was about to meet them both at his office. They were referred to him by a great friend, so it confused him even more. Q was past livid now. He was so furious that he was calm, and he knew this meant things were about to get crazy.

He walked into his deli that led to his office. This was the only business he owned in Brooklyn. For years he was paying the deli owner to use his basement because it was low and discreet and of course, money talks.

About a year ago the original owner passed away from old age. To Q's surprise he left his deli to him in his will. He renamed it *Q's Spot*. He was doing great for himself and he was happy, until three days ago before his world started crashing down with the news of Toya's death. He walked inside, greeted his employee, and told him he could go home early, he'd close the shop up himself. Q handed him $300 for the pay he would miss.

Q was genuine and he showed loved. He never forgot where he came from and he never let the money change him. This was a major reason why he moved the way he did in the streets. He was about his family and his business.

He turned the lights out, put the closed banner up and locked the doors. He went to the side door and made sure it was unlocked. He walked to the back of the deli by the freezer section and moved a rack of chips over to the left. Behind it was the door to his office and it required a code to open. He punched in his code and walked downstairs.

His office was very spacious, it was the size of a small lounge. The walls were dark, concrete and soundproof, and the floor was dark marble. One section of his office had some of his favorite quotes graffitied on the walls in fancy blue letters.

A lot of "other" type of business went on in the office but you would never know unless you knew. Although it was a basement, it was set up like an actual office. He had a nice black desk that was in the shape of a piano and black Sunpan, Bugatti Grain, Leather couches. He loved the color black.

Q went to his weapon safe, which stood almost to the ceiling. He admired all of his guns before he picked out his 9mm and kissed it. He knew shit was about to get hectic.

His phone rang and he knew it had to be Frankie and Rico. He picked up and said come in before he hung up the phone. About 4 minutes later, he heard his bell ring.

Very few people knew the code to get pass the door and very few people knew about the door even being there. Q tried to move as smart as possible when it came to keeping his business on the low. He buzzed them in and they walked downstairs. Q was sitting at his desk with his leg crossed and his right hand grooming his beard calmly.

"What's wrong boss? What happened?" Frankie immediately asked, standing in front of Q's desk. Q liked Frankie, he was always ready to put in work with no problem and he finished the job extra smoothly. Unfortunately though, this wasn't about who Q liked anymore. He had his sister's blood on his own hands.

"So, who took care of the girl from the other day?" Q asked, trying to keep a stern voice even though he was sick to his stomach.

"I did boss," Rico said proudly. "It was nice and quiet," he added. Q couldn't show any emotion through his face as Rico spoke, he was in go mode.

"*How* did you kill her?" Q asked.

"I put a bullet right between her eyes boss," Rico said confidently.

Each of Rico's answers made Q's blood hot. He stood up out of his chair and walked over in front of Rico. He pulled his gun out and shot him point blank range between his eyes. Rico died instantly and his body hit the marble floor hard. Frankie froze. He didn't expect this to happen at all.

"Yo! What the fuck?!" he asked changing his tone from loud to low when he saw Q point his gun at him.

"Yo, yo boss man! What's going on? Please! Wait a minute! Wait! Wait!" he started pleading with his hands up.

"I like you Frankie, I like the way you move, but don't *EVER* fucking question me!" Q said with a straight serious face and tone.

"Sorry boss, I'm just, I-I don't know I'm n-nervous man. Did I do something wrong?" he asked hoping that wasn't considered questioning him.

"No, no you did everything right Frankie, you did everything fucking right. It's a good thing you had Rico do the job because if not, that would be you right there," Q said pointing to Rico's lifeless body and brains on the floor. "You see, those pictures you sent me... that's my sister and my bitch. Well, my ex-bitch. I had no fucking idea that's who was robbing me," Q said, walking in a circle around Frankie now and talking almost as if he was talking to himself. "So, in other words Frankie, I put a hit out on my own peoples. The funeral that you were planning on going to, that's for my sister. I would have been right at the same fucking funeral."

Q was pissed. "Do you see where I'm going with this?" Q stopped walking and stood directly in front of Frankie waiting for a response. Frankie didn't say a word. "Good answer," Q whispered in Frankie's face. Q's eyes were so wide that Frankie could see the white of his eyes around the entire perimeter of his iris. He could tell that Q was not in his right state of mind.

"Do you know how I feel right now Frankie?" Q asked. Frankie was still quiet. Although he wanted to speak, he thought it would be best if he did not. "Nah I know you don't. You have no fucking idea how I feel right now. You think I wanted to kill Rico? How long that nigga been down with me?" he continued.

Q threw his hands up as he spoke, "I had to kill him Frankie, you know why?" Q was talking sarcastic and crazy. "Because he killed my fucking sister. I already gotta live with the fact that it's *my* fault. But, do you think I could live with seeing the nigga's face every day that did it? *Nahhh,* not gonna happen!" Q was still walking around as he was talking.

"You know Frankie, I think there's a reason Rico handled it and not you. I think you were meant to help me figure this shit out. Now, I'm not 100% sure if they knew it was me they were robbing or not. I think there's a snake around that was somehow setting everything up. I don't know yet. I want you to find out. So, what do you say Frankie? You ridin' or dyin'?" Q stopped in front of Frankie's face again, looking him right in the eyes, waiting for him to answer.

"I'm riding boss" Frankie said with a straight face and loyal heart. After hearing what was going on Frankie understood more of why Q did what he did. He didn't know if he would have handled it the way Q did if it was him, but he respected it.

"That's what I like to hear Frankie," Q said patting Frankie on the back. "Now this is what we gonna do," Q put his hand on Frankie shoulder and started telling him the plan. After talking, they dug a hole outside in the back and buried Rico's body together. Q left his office with vengeance in his soul...

CHAPTER SEVEN

Kim tried her hardest to keep herself busy to stay out of her thoughts, but it just wasn't working. She had gotten her hair and nails done and picked her outfit out for the funeral. The funeral was the next morning and she was going to open up to Q about everything, or at least that's what she told herself. She didn't know if Q would still look at her in the same light afterwards, and she wasn't ready to handle that.

The truth of the matter was Toya & Kim were larcenists. To make matters worse, they became murderers. Until this day, Kim still could not believe they got away with so much dirt. She hated to admit it, but she knew after a while that karma would come back to the both of them. Aside from knowing this, it still did not justify the broken heart she carried from the loss of her friend. Since Toya's been gone, she regretted every day that they ever got involved with this shit.

A few years back, Toya and Kim were chillin'. It was a summer day and they were sitting outside of their apartment complex, doing their regular thing. It was never quiet in Brooklyn and something was always going on, especially when it was hot. It was as if the heat just made people act up.

Kim would never forget this day. A shiny green Cadillac with gold spinning wheels pulled up blasting Trick Daddy the rapper. It caused Toya and Kim both to do a double take because cars like that weren't coming up and down their block too often.

"Who the hell is that?" Toya asked Kim.

"Girl, I have no idea but shiiit, I need his number," Kim laughed. She was always the fast friend and Toya would either give her approval or not. She never judged.

They watched as this tall man with a jerry curl in his hair got out of the car looking around as if someone was hiding from him. They watched closely as he walked up and down the block screaming for someone named Candie. When they saw the girl come from the back of the building half-dressed, they figured out what was going on. Candie must've been a PS (short for pussy seller or prostitute) and this guy must've been her pimp.

Toya and Kim never thought about prostituting, but they often thought about how much money they heard the good girls made. The pimp had to feel them staring because he turned around and stared back before pointing over at them.

A few minutes later, the girl who the pimp referred to as Candie started strutting over to them, Toya and Kim both looked at each other with confused faces wondering what she wanted.

"What's up girls? I'm Candie, my friend over there said he likes what he sees. If y'all two wanna get down, making some *good* money, give him a call."

She tried to hand Toya a card, but she didn't take it. Kim reached out, snatched the card and simply said "aight." Candie turned around and walked back over to her pimp.

Kim had her eyes closed while she replayed this day over. She started hitting herself in the head with the palm of her hand, *why the hell did I take that damn card* she asked herself.

About a week after taking the card from Candie, they decided to call her pimp. His name was Slick and he had a tight line up of females in New Jersey. His attitude was very hard and stern. His girls were very pretty and well kept. Kim and Toya fit right in if not stood out. Now they weren't willing to fuck for the money, but they were willing to front and take the money. They thought that if they could get Slick to put them on, they could round up their own customers and do their own thing. And that's just what they did.

Their first time on the strip was interesting. It was them and four other girls. They were staying in a fancy hotel with a beautiful view. Instead of standing on corners, they were standing around in the bars of the

Hotel waiting around for a customer. So many old white men were in the bars drunk and lonely, looking for any pretty girl to chat with. Toya and Kim had their first "date," as they called it, together. They convinced a fat white man to pay them $1,600 just to dance and strip with each other. At first, they were a little unsure, but then they thought about how they got dressed in front of each other all the time. This time they just had to touch on each other a little bit. It wasn't hard to touch on a pretty girl for money they thought, especially your best friend.

When they checked into the room, they took a few shots of liquor and smoked some weed before starting. They wanted to loosen up and calm their nerves. They played their own music until their customer came in. He requested a weird, white singer that they had never heard of. It turned them off, but they wanted the money.

While they were dancing and stripping, the old man started jerking off. He never mentioned this being a part of the plan, but it was too late now. They both looked at him disgusted, they decided to just stare at each other and tune him out. The old man jerked himself harder and harder and moaned as Toya and Kim continued to dance for him.

"Come closer," the fat white man said to them. They looked at each other to see if they were both on the same page. They nodded to each other and moved onto the bed with the man never letting their eyes leave each other's. They kept dancing and touching on each other.

"Ahhhhh," the man screamed out while still jerking off and cumin at the same time. He pointed his white slim penis at Kim first and shot nut on her titties. He moved his penis to Toya now getting cum on her face. They felt disrespected.

Toya and Kim became closer after that evening, they shared their deepest darkest secrets together. After this night, they decided that they would definitely go in to business for themselves. It made no sense to them. Paying Slick so much of their earnings when they could be their own bosses.

For a long time, they would meet up with lonely old men that were willing to pay thousands sometimes for all the nasty shit they would promise they would do to them. They would be the ones in charge now. They would be the ones who would decide what the men were allowed and not allowed to do. Anything that was done extra and wasn't discussed from the beginning of the conversation would cost a penalty fee. They made rules and they made sure their customers knew. They had it all set up to where they'd find them on low down social sites and then, hit them up from burner phones. These were disposable phones that they would change up every week or so. It was harder for these phones to be traced; just in case anything went wrong.

One thing they made sure of was that they left no traces of evidence. They made sure to never deal with anyone in or close to their hometown. Everything was done out of town. They would disguise themselves so well that sometimes, the makeup would change their complexion. They would meet their victims in hotel rooms under fake names, drug them and then take the money the men planned on paying for their service, along with whatever other valuables they came with.

They were surprised by some of the things that the men carried. They took everything down to their credit cards and jewelry. They drugged so many men it became boring. They never hurt anyone, aside from their victim's pockets. They didn't worry too much about the men calling the police because prostitution was illegal and that's exactly what this looked like.

Their favorite part of their plan was shopping afterwards, but even that became boring when they realized they had more clothes and shoes than they could wear. All the money they made they blew on hairstyles, clothes, and partying. After a while, they realized they should've been moving smarter. They needed a car, a house, real shit.

Just when they decided they would hit just a few more jabs and then leave this life alone for good, Kim met Ty during one of their "jobs." It just so happened that one of their victims was also a major drug lord. He was in town for the weekend for business and wanted to have some fun. Toya and Kim didn't find this out until it was too late. They drugged their victim and before they could finish searching all of his belongings, the room door was kicked in. This caught them both off guard and they ran to the closet to grab their guns. They were always prepared, just in case things got ugly.

"Woah, woah! Don't move," Ty said to Kim. "What the fuck are y'all doing here and what happened to this clown?" he asked as if they knew each other and were going to tell the truth. Surprisingly Kim did.

"Look, we're some hookers without the hook up. We drugged this fool and got paid for our services. Whatever business you got going on with him, we don't know nothing about and don't want no parts. We got our shit and we wanna dip. We're strapped too." Kim pointed to Toya holding her gun and ready to use it.

Ty was shocked and turned on. "Oh, so y'all some stick up bitches? Well, we some stick up niggas and we're here for the drugs," he said seriously.

"Look, we don't know nothin' bout no drugs. Everything this cracker came with is over there," Kim said as she pointed to the victim's belongings in the corner.

"Go check that out" Ty told one of his men. His man opened the duffle bags and they were both filled with heroin as expected. "So, this is the type of shit you into huh?" Ty asked Kim trying to flirt. She repeated the question back to him.

"So, this the type of shit you into huh," she said with an attitude.

"Yeah, grown men shit. When you ready to make some real chedda in this line of work, without dressing up like a half-naked clown, holla at me." Ty handed his card to Kim.

She knew he was referring to her make up by calling her a clown. "I'm probably the sexiest half naked clown you've ever seen in your entire life, fuck boy," she said to Ty as she snatched the card and left the room with Toya.

Who the fuck did he think he was she said to herself as she looked down at the card. *Imma still call his ass though* she thought as she smiled and put the card in her bra.

It took Kim a week or two to call Ty. Toya wasn't really with it. She wanted to stick to their plan and drug a few more men until they had enough money to do what they needed to do.

Kim started to feel horrible now. Toya wanted out and she only continued because of her loyalty to Kim. Before they started to work for Ty he made it very clear that no one was to be left alive during these robberies. If this rule was ever broken, they would be permanently removed from this line of work. Permanently meant death. They've lied, drugged, and robbed for the money but were they ready to kill for it? They had a lot to think about.

Ty had everything set up for them before they would hit a punch. He would tell them when and where they would meet the men and how it would go down. They never knew who they were robbing, they just followed the plan that Ty set up for them. Ty felt that the less they knew the better. He was from out of town and wanted to stay as low as possible. He made sure that most of the time it was only one man that they had to take down.

There were only a few times that they had to take down two. This last robbery went completely wrong. They fucked up and left a person alive and still took the money. Kim knew this is why Toya was dead.

Ty put a hit out on them because they broke the rules. Kim also thought maybe Ty wanted them dead because they knew too much. Either way she had to tell Q before they found her. She still had no idea how she was going to tell him about her grimy lifestyle. She was a murderer and a thief, Q hated thieves. He always looked at them as cowards.

Kim couldn't imagine Q finding out the person he's in love with and thought he knew everything about was a cold-blooded thief and murderer. How could she ask him to defend her in so much wrong?

Kim started to feel like she deserved to be dead with Toya again. She started thinking of other options besides telling Q the truth. Her mind went to thoughts of the detective and quickly left, *no snitching* she told herself. *Maybe I could take the money and disappear for good after the funeral*, she thought to herself. It's not like Toya was around for her to miss, she started thinking to herself. Now she was confused and didn't know what the hell she was going to do.

CHAPTER EIGHT

Q was stuck. He was confused and he couldn't understand for the life of him how or why any of this was happening. He was ready to get to the bottom of this. He had faith in Frankie and was hoping he'd hear some good news from him soon.

Now, he was on his way home to face Kim. He asked himself over and over, wondering how he would handle this. He didn't want Kim to know what he knew right away. He had to get his mind right first. *Damn was she even going to tell me?* He questioned himself. He had too many unanswered questions and he honestly didn't know if he could sit around Kim and pretend that he didn't know any longer.

Q loved everything about Kim. If he was to ever get married, she would be his bride. Now here he was, thinking she was an angel, thinking he knew everything about her, thinking she never kept any secrets, and she was living a grimy double lifestyle. How was it that she kept this from Q and only showed her delicate side, he wondered? He felt stupid. Q didn't mind the murders so much, he had some skeletons in his closet too, but the robberies threw him off.

To take from people you had to be grimy. To kill someone because you're taking from them, you had to be a grimy snake, and he couldn't have any snakes around him. *But damn Kim, were you really a snake?* He thought to himself. *And Toya, damn T, you were into this shit too? You were closer to me. You were my sister.* Q's thoughts were all over and his head was hurting. He had no idea how he was about to be next to this bitch without tripping.

Upon arriving to his residence, he ordered his butler to leave for the evening, telling him that he wanted some privacy for the night. He sat in the dark waiting for Kim as he thought about all of his solutions. He knew that if he killed Kim, he would miss her deeply, but he was already missing Toya like crazy. He didn't think it was fair that Kim continued to live while Toya didn't. "FUCK!" he screamed out loud as he made himself upset. He was so angry about this whole situation and he knew he didn't have it in him to kill Kim. Kim was his bitch and he couldn't see himself hurting her. *Imma choke this girl until she comes clean.* He thought to himself. *Nah I might make a mistake and kill her. Think, think, think, Q THINK.* His mind was all over the place.

He got up and walked to the bathroom to splash some water on his face. "You gone act like nothing's wrong and you gone stick to the plan," he told himself while looking into the mirror. He took a deep breath and headed back into the living room to wait for Kim.

A knock at Q's door startled him. He wasn't expecting company and he had given Kim a key after all this bullshit started. He grabbed his gun from his nightstand drawer and walked over to the door, looking through the peephole. It was black as if someone was covering it with their hand.

"Who is it?" Q asked in a deep voice.

"My name is Detective White. I'm looking for a Qazir Jones," Detective White stated.

"What for?" Q asked confused. One thing he never associated himself with was police. He didn't welcome any type of contact with them. He was confused about how they even got his address.

"I would like to ask you some questions regarding Toya Richards. I'm investigating her case and I know you two were close. Could you please open the door?" the detective said sounding desperate.

Q took a deep breath relieved that she was here for Toya and not anything else. He thought twice before he let her in. He didn't have anything to tell her, but that didn't mean she wouldn't have something to tell him, Q thought as he decided to open the door. He turned his lights back on and placed his gun in his pants behind his back as he invited the detective inside.

When he saw her, he was shocked to see she was so pretty and looked so young. Most detectives around his way were either old and miserable or young and bitter.

"Thank you," detective White spoke as she looked Q up and down. She'd seen plenty of men in her field of work, but she's never found any of them attractive. She kept her composure and remained professional.

"What could I do for you, Officer White?" Q asked getting straight to the point.

"Well, as I said before Mr. Jones, I'm investigating the murder of Toya Richards. I know you and her were very close according to her mom. I just wanted to know if you had *any* idea of who could have wanted to hurt her?" Detective White felt like she was repeating herself over and over with this question, but she had to ask.

"Officer, honestly, if I knew the motherfuckers who did this to my sister, I'd be taking their life away as we speak," Q was brutally honest with the detective.

Detective White cleared her throat, "Well, Mr. Jones thank you for your honesty," she didn't know what else to say to him.

"Can I ask you a question? Do you have any leads or motives yet? I know a lot of cases around here are given up on when it comes to black people in the ghetto," Q said with a hint of sarcasm.

"Well, actually Mr. Jones, we came across money that was sort of "put away" in Ms. Richards apartment, if you know what I mean. It was a large sum of money and I couldn't help but to think that maybe someone was trying to rob her. Maybe they couldn't find it and acted out in a fit of rage. I don't know Mr. Jones. I am trying to figure it out," she spoke to Q in a tired manner as if she was ready to give up.

Q's mind was racing a mile a minute after Detective White mentioned the money. *What if that's my money*, he thought. Q wondered how much money the detective was speaking about, but he knew if he asked her it would draw attention to himself. *Damn*, he thought. Now that the detective had the money, he wondered if she would be looking more into things. *This could definitely be bad for business,* Q thought.

"I don't know who would want to hurt her and if she had money, I'm sure she was probably saving up for something. I wish I could help more detective, but I can't. Now no offense but I have a busy night," Q walked over to the door and opened it to see Detective White out. She left without a word. She wasn't getting help from anyone and she realized she would have to get to the bottom of this on her own.

Q closed his door and took a deep breath. Things were getting more and more out of control. He had to hurry up and get to the bottom of this. He turned his lights back off and waited for Kim.

When Kim got to Q's it was quiet and dark. There was usually at least one person around and at least one light on. It was unusual but she paid no attention to it. Everything seemed unusual since this nightmare started. She put her bags down in the living room, they were heavy and she had been walking for miles while carrying them. When she walked into Q's room it was pitch black. She tried to flick the light switch on, but it didn't work. She knew her way around the room, so it wasn't hard for her to make it to the nightstand using her hands.

"Come here." Q's voice startled her and made her jump.

"Oh, shit Q! Don't do that nigga!" she said feeling a little less tense now.

"Just come here," he said firmly. She started walking towards Q's voice. She felt him sitting in the recliner in the corner and she sat on his lap.

Her body felt a little hot when she felt his manhood. It's been years since her and Q fucked. They connected every other way, mind, mental, and soul but they made a promise they'd keep the intimate part out. None of that mattered now to Kim. This was her nigga, and if they got through this nightmare together, she was throwing all the bullshit in her life away and settling down with her man.

"How you doing? I haven't really been able to ask since this bad news," Q asked Kim.

"Q, I don't know if I'm coming or going. I'm just here," Kim said in a crackling voice.

"It's aight, I got something for you, drink this." Q put a shot glass to Kim's lips and made her throw it back. Kim coughed a little. The shot of henny felt good, but it was strong. It sent a heated shock through her body. Q gave her another one and another one. Before she knew it, she had taken seven shots and was feeling a little loose.

Q grabbed Kim's face with both his hands. He could tell the liquor was kicking in but it would probably take another half hour for the pills he slipped in it to work. He was staring at Kim while holding her face, *look at this beautiful snake,* he thought to himself. He started kissing her hard and rough. He slowly slid his right hand down from the side of her face to her neck, squeezing it lightly. His light squeeze turned tighter as he kissed her harder and harder. Kim let out a little moan. Q was being rough but she liked it. She figured he needed to let some of his anger and frustration out. Not to mention her hormones had been rising due to pregnancy.

His grip stayed tight around her neck and he stood up lifting her almost off her toes. He pinned her up against the wall holding her left arm up by her elbow. He let go of her neck and slid his hand roughly over her face and up into her hair. He pulled her hair as he slid his hand down her head and back to her neck. He bit her neck hard and long. Whatever pleasure he gave her tonight he wanted to add pain.

Kim was loving it. Her head was spinning, her body was hot, and her little friend between her legs had a heartbeat. She was ready for Q to fuck her right then and there on the wall, but he had other plans. He slid his hands under her shirt and grabbed her firm breast tight and rough almost squeezing her nipple off.

Q whispered in her ear, "you ready to suck some dick?" Kim moaned and grabbed Qs cock, wanting to show him how ready she was.

She didn't know what came over her, if it was the liquor, the stress she needed to relieve, or just the thought of how much she missed fucking Q.

"Slow down now," Q said to Kim with a grin on his face. Kim was always a freak, but she was extra freaky for Q, and he loved that about her.

One of the main reasons they decided to stop fucking was because he knew she would have him out here going crazy when it came to her being with other niggas. So, they kept the love in their relationship but took the sex out. Q walked over to his bed, leading Kim by her arm. He sat down and told her to get on her knees. Kim did as she was told and went to unzip his pants, eager to give him head. Q slapped Kim jokingly but firmly enough for her to know he was serious.

"Did daddy say to touch it?" he asked, looking at Kim's shocked face. He's never put his hands on her before, so he knew she was caught off guard.

Kim was startled after the slap but for the strangest reason, she loved it. He wanted to be in control and although she usually took the lead when it came to him, she allowed him to have his power for now.

"Daddy can I touch it?" she asked in a sultry seductive voice, pouting her face as if she was begging.

"Say please," Q told her.

"Daddy can I touch it pleeeaaase?" Kim dragged her please as if she was a kid asking for a lollipop. Q nodded his head yes and watched as Kim snatched his dick out of his pants as if it was her first meal of a long day. She went to work. Q almost gave in but he wanted to run the show so he took control. He grabbed Kim's face while she was sucking and started moving it up and down slowly.

"You like that?" he asked as he started moving her face faster. Kim couldn't respond. Her mouth was full. "I said do you like that?" Q asked again sternly, moving her face back and forth even harder than before now. Kim started choking while trying to speak so she moaned out "yes" the best that she could. "I can't hear you," Q stopped moving her head back and forth now and held her face down forcing himself to the back of her throat. Kim moaned out *"yes"* the best she could again, only this time it was also the loudest that she could.

She was feeling a little weird. Q was rough, but this wasn't like him. She looked up at him and saw him staring right at her, with a look in his eyes that she had never seen before.

"What you looking at? Keep sucking," Q told her as he started to move her face up and down again. Kim shed a tear. She didn't know if it was from pleasure or nervousness, but she kept sucking as she was told.

After about a half hour of being on her knees, Kim was ready to stop. She looked up at Q and thought to herself if she should. He had his head back now and it looked as if he was enjoying himself. *Maybe he's about to cum, I'm not gone stop yet*, Kim said to herself. Sure enough a few minutes later Q came all over Kim's face. He usually felt like this was a way of making a female his bitch, but this time he wanted it to mean disrespect. If this was going to be his last time fucking Kim, he wanted to make it epic.

"Take your clothes off," he told her as he watched her strip. He could tell from her pupils that his pills had kicked in. He gave her two, triple-stack Gladys which was a high dose of ecstasy. By the morning she wouldn't remember any of this.

Q reached over to his nightstand and turned the light on. He wanted to be able to see her naked body. She was beautiful in bare form. Q's emotions started getting the best of him again. He didn't know what to do with her. He shook it off, threw her on the bed and told her to put her ass in the air. Kim flew on the bed as if she weighed only 10 lbs. She had no control over her body and she knew something was wrong. She did as she was told and put her ass in the air.

Q took his time before he slid inside of her. It had been a while since he had Kim like this and it was probably going to be the last time. He slid into her tight vagina slow and firm. Kim let out a gasp that she didn't know was in her. She felt like she was going to cum just from his entry. She remembered why she agreed to stop fucking him as long as they weren't official. His dick was too bomb and it would have her wildin' out over a nigga that ain't officially hers.

He started with slow strokes before he started pounding on Kim's pussy. He had no remorse and ignored her screams of him to stop by putting a pillow over her head. He didn't have it in his heart to kill Kim or to even physically abuse her, so the next best thing to him was to do it sexually. He fucked her until she passed out.

CHAPTER NINE

Kim woke up, slowly trying to remember who she was. She had a pounding headache as if she had a hangover but she couldn't remember from what. When she opened her eyes and tried to use her hands to rub them, she realized she was tied down to a chair. *What the fuck,* she thought to herself. She was still out of it and couldn't panic if she wanted to.

She tried to move her legs and realized they were also tied to the chair. She couldn't figure out what the hell was going on. It was dark and cold wherever she was, and she felt it in her bones. She was in a real bad situation.

Who the fuck kidnapped me she thought to herself. *Oh shit,* her thoughts clicked, *it's gotta be Ty's people.* Kim just knew she was about to die, *I let these motherfuckers catch me first, fuck!* She was livid. *How the fuck did they even get me*, she tried to figure out. She took a deep breath and tried to remember. *Q! I was with Q!, oh shit they got Q*! Kim started to panic. She didn't have the exact time, but she knew that if it was the next day, it was the day of her best friend's funeral. Her man was probably dead or somewhere hurting, and she was tied to a chair in somebody's fucking basement. Her mind went to Ty, *I should've never fucked with that sleaze ball*!

Kim thought about how much she liked Ty. She never would have imagined that they would end up where they were now. She knew she shouldn't have mixed business with pleasure, but Ty was fine as hell and his rough, rugged attitude turned her on. He was six foot three, golden brown, with nice, neat and thick dreads down to his back. His shoulders were perfectly toned, not too brocky, not too frail, and he was tatted up. Ty had this mysterious look to him and that's what Kim fell for. She thought she could figure him out.

She started to think about the first job her and Toya ever did for Ty. It was around two weeks after she took his card from him. Before he allowed them to "join the team" as he would say, he told them he wanted to get to know more of what they were about. He invited them both out to Long Island to spend a weekend with him and his friend at a hotel.

At first, Kim thought he was just trying to set up a double date and she honestly did not mind. She soon learned however that he only wanted to give them the complete run down of the operation in person.

Everything about Ty that weekend was screaming for Kim to fuck with him. The way he took charge and demanded obedience touched something in her. She was stuck on lust when it came to him.

Days before their first scheduled job, Toya became nervous.

"Kim, we ain't never kill nobody before girl. You sure we can do this?" Kim looked at Toya surprised; she's never seen fear in her friend's eyes before. All Kim could think about was the money. She ignored the sincere look of dismay on her friends face and told her, "It's okay T, we're gonna be good. We went over the plan a million times. We know what to do. It's just one man we gotta take down then boom, we're a couple thousand richer." Kim sounded so sure she almost surprised herself. She was speaking as if she had done this before.

"What if shit don't go right Kim? What if this nigga is setting us up? Can we even trust him?" Toya overthought although she had a valid point. Kim ignored the fact that she could be right. She just wanted to hit the lick and get paid.

"This nigga done told us too much already girl. He would have killed us when he first saw us if it was like that." Kim continued trying to convince Toya that everything was going to be fine.

About 10 more minutes into the conversation, they were both back on the same page. They agreed to work for Ty only a few times to get their money right and then leave this shit alone for good.

The day of their first job, they were both more than ready. Toya no longer brought up "what if's" and they had their game faces on. They did exactly what Ty told them to do. They were in the hotel room where the drop was supposed to take place. Hiding in the closet, they listened as the meeting went down between two men. One had the drugs and the other had the money. The voices Ty told them they would hear they heard, the same conversation that Ty told them would take place between the two voices took place.

Down to the exact time that Ty told them, one of the voices would exit the room. It was completely on que. Everything was smooth just as he said it would be. Toya and Kim locked eyes in the dark closet, it was show time. They both closed their eyes then kissed their hands to God. Kim pushed her side of the closet door open first. She startled the person that was still in the room, he was completely caught off guard. Kim pointed her gun at his face as they looked at each other. *Am I really going to kill this nigga?* She was questioning herself now.

"WHERE'S THE MONEY?" she asked firmly. Kim's victim was quiet. She asked him again for the money this time putting the gun into his mouth.

"It's over there," the guy said in a heavy Spanish accent. Toya came out of the closet suddenly causing the man to jump, he had no idea that there were two of them. She went and grabbed the bag their victim said the cash was in. She opened the bag and her eyes lit up. This was more money than they'd ever made while being hookers, and it was just one hit.

"You don't know who you're *fucking* with miss!" said the victim as Toya closed the bag back up and put it on her shoulder.

"Neither do you," Kim replied in an evil tone before she pulled the trigger and shot the man through his mouth. Her silencer on the gun she used from Ty kept their transaction discreet.

She hurried and checked the room to make sure no traces were left behind. They did as they were told and left the room the same way they came. They both remained silent until they got back to their own motel room. It was low key and not too far. The jobs would mostly be out of town, so it required them to stay for two days, checking in the night before.

Back in their motel room, Kim snatched her wig off, ran to the bathroom and instantly threw up. She felt sick and her body was shaking. She couldn't believe that she had just taken someone's life and watched them while doing it. Toya walked over to her and rubbed her back.

"You aight sis?" Toya asked nervously, concerned for her friend.

"I killed somebody T," Kim replied as she looked at the gun that she still had on her. "I just took someone's life," was all Kim said.

Toya watched her as her eyes changed. Her crying and worry turned into laughs.

"I just fucking shot somebody," Kim was laughing like a lunatic now holding the gun in the air. Toya watched as her friend transformed into some kind of pretty little monster. Toya felt concerned but she brushed it off.

"Kim, we're in this shit together. I got your back forever and you know our secrets are safe with us," she reassured her friend before hugging her. From that job on, Kim had always been the first one to shoot. She was on some type of power trip since her first murder.

The next day Kim called Ty to let him know their status.

"What's up Kim Kim?" Ty answered the phone on the third ring. She loved the way he flirted with her.

"That suit that you asked me to drop off to the cleaners is finished and ready for pick up," Kim spoke in code. She was referring to the job being done and their money being picked up.

"Oh yeah? That's great news, I wanted to wear it tonight to dinner. Pick up the suit for me please and bring it to me later." Ty played along with Kim. He told her where and when to meet him so they could exchange the money.

Kim wanted to look extra pretty when she arrived at the location Ty requested. She wanted Ty and she wanted him to know that. She was tired of the mixed signals he gave her all the time. She was going to let it be known that she wanted him and she was going to have him.

"I'm going to meet Ty alone tonight," Kim told Toya as she hung up the phone.

"What you mean alone? Let me find out," Toya laughed as she nudged her friend with her elbow.

"Girl I want him. I've been wanting him, and tonight is the night," Kim laughed back with her friend. "Now come on help me fix my hair up."

A few hours later, Kim was all ready to get her hands-on Ty. She was back in town and she had dropped Toya off at home. She was standing in her bedroom admiring herself in her full-length, wall mirror. Her long, pretty hair was half up, half down with curls and her red lipstick added to her beauty. She wore a tight figure fitting black dress with black heels. She went over her eye liner one last time and waited for her cell to ring.

It was 7:45pm and Ty said he would be ready to leave by 8. She sprayed her *Guess for Women* perfume by Elizabeth Arden on her wrist and behind her ears. She grabbed her black trench coat and headed out the door. She figured she would get some gas while waiting on

Ty's call. She knew the drive to him would be at least two hours.

Like clockwork, her phone rang after getting gas and a water.

"Did you pick the suit up sexy?" Ty asked with his masculine voice. Kim blushed but she remained calm. Ty was being extra flirty tonight.

"Yes, I did and I'm ready to give it to you," Kim flirted back.

"Good because I need it. You know where dinner is. I'm on my way now," Ty hung up the phone just like that. Kim was tingling, *oh he needs it huh she thought to herself.* She looked into her rearview mirror and smiled. It was about to be a great night she thought. She drove out of the gas station and headed to the freeway. She blasted Red Light Special by one of her favorite girl groups, TLC.

Kim shook her head from this memory and came back to reality. Thinking about how what happened felt as if she was reliving it. It felt so real. She looked around and everything was dark. She tried hard again to remember what happened and how she got here but she couldn't. All she remembered was going back to Q's. Her mind drifted to Q more, she loved him. He was the only man she had ever given her heart to. Everyone else was just boy toys to her. Ty was her favorite one, *Ty,* she thought. Her mind went back to the night after their first job as she closed her eyes in the dark.

When she reached the destination Ty had given her, it was a beautiful hotel with an ocean view. The room was filled with black and purple rose petals thrown around everywhere. From the dressers, to the bed, to the floor, they coated the room beautifully. Candles complemented the petals, lighting up the walkway. *I must be in the wrong damn room*, Kim thought to herself. *I know this nigga ain't do all of this*, she thought and smiled as she closed the door and placed her duffle bags in the closet.

She walked further into the room to see Ty sitting on the couch. *He looks almost as good as me*, Kim thought to herself as she admired Ty's attire. He was wearing a grey, fitted, business suit with a crisp, white, button up underneath with grey and black cufflinks. His dreads were freshly twisted into rows as if they were braids. His shape up looked lickable to Kim. He was playing the part of going to a "fancy dinner" beyond well. He looked like dirty money to Kim. Just what she liked.

"You did all of this for me? Or one of your hoes coming through after I dip?" Kim asked Ty flirtingly but serious.

Ty smirked, "I always liked your smart-ass mouth Kim. I wonder what else it's good at," he insulted her in a flirtatious way.

Kim took no offense at all. "I can show you, so you don't gotta wonder no more, boss man."

Kim looked at Ty in a seductive way and he looked at her the same. He stood up and walked over to Kim, placing his hands on her shoulders.

"Why don't you take this off and stay awhile," he whispered in her ear as he slowly slid her coat off of her shoulders. His warm whispers were turning Kim on. She closed her eyes as he slid his fingers down her soft arm while removing her coat.

"And yeah, I did all of this for you. You my hoe for the night," he slapped her ass and admired the reverb. He walked off to put her coat in the closet.

Kim's panties were soaked, and she could feel it. The way Ty called her his hoe made her wanna grab his dick and pull it out right there. She kept her composure not to seem thirsty. She walked behind him joining him on the balcony.

"Well since you did all of this for me how about I thank you before dinner," Kim said as she rubbed her hand over Ty's crotch. His dick was even bigger than she imagined, and it was still sleeping.

Ty smiled. He pulled his gun out and startled Kim. She took a step back as he pointed it at her, she felt stupid for a second. She was completely indefensible. She had not one weapon on her. She had left everything in her car.

"Can I trust you Kim?" Ty asked as he placed the gun on the table. Kim was still a little nervous, but she kept herself calm.

"I just killed someone for you, I think it's a little too late to ask me that now," Kim answered with her usual smart mouth.

"I just thought I'd ask. I saw what you and your friend were about at the hotel, but this here is big man business. As I told you before, any mistakes and its lights out for the both of you," Ty spoke with so much sincerity in his voice, he meant his words.

"I don't think I'm gonna have an issue with you though. That's why I gave you my card. You gone be my number one," Ty smiled. He could tell everything he was saying to Kim was sinking in.

"Now, I thought I heard you say something about thanking me earlier," Ty laughed and took his suit jacket off. He sat down on the bench and placed his hands behind his head. *Oh, this nigga think he the man huh*, Kim thought as she looked Ty up and down wanting to take his clothes off. *I'm gonna be number one huh*, she smiled. She loved the aggressor in Ty, but she didn't like the fact that he thought he had to fill her head up.

Number one she thought, *we are not in high school*. She picked up a drink that Ty had out on a beautifully made table with dinner. She looked around outside as the fresh air blew through her hair, the lights made the night more pleasing. She walked back inside and turned on the stereo in the room. She went to her playlist and started with Doing It Well by LL Cool J. Now she was ready. All she needed was two more drinks.

Walking back out to the balcony she started to remove her dress. She gave Ty a strip tease as she watched the bulge in his crotch area grow. She was standing with her back towards Ty now, completely bending over removing her dress and shaking her ass at the same time. Ty was standing up now, he couldn't keep sitting. He wanted to touch on Kim. He slapped her ass as she kept shaking it. She turned around facing him now and looking into his eyes. She walked up to him and licked his neck. This caused Ty to moan, turning Kim on more. He tried to kiss her and she turned her face, she didn't kiss niggas.

She unbuttoned his shirt and ripped it off his arms. She rubbed her hands all over his tatted chest and started to kiss it. She kissed his chest down to his waist. Getting down on her knees now she looked him in the eye as she unbuttoned his pants.

"Is there something in here for me?" she asked Ty in a baby voice. Ty was completely turned on and into Kim. He was ready to bend her over and pound her out but he was letting her do her thing. He was enjoying it anyway.

"There might be. Why don't you find out?" Ty said to Kim, rubbing his fingers over her lips. Kim smiled as she pulled his pants and underwear down and had him standing completely naked on the balcony. She licked his hard and firm penis up and down before touching it. She licked up and down and teased him by sucking the tip, then letting it go. She had her hand on his dick now while sucking it. She sucked and sucked and let it grow more and more down her throat.

Ty had his hand in Kim's hair now, pushing her head up and down on his dick. Kim looked up at him while she let him take control of her head. Coming up for air now, Kim was jerking Ty off with her hand. She spit on his dick while jerking it and then sucked it up.

She was being extra nasty with Ty. The liquor was kicking in and LL's voice through the speaker made the scene more fascinating. She felt like she really was *doing it well* on the balcony with Ty's fine ass. She put both of his balls in her mouth and sucked them softly. She started sucking again, putting his whole penis in her throat. She sucked and deep throated Ty like a porn star.

Ty pulled her up by her neck and tried to kiss her again. This time Kim kissed him, she surprised herself but him wanting to taste himself turned her on. They kissed each other long and deep. Ty ripped Kim's bra off and started licking over each of her nipples. He saw this aroused her so he started to suck them, sucking each one softly and then firmly. Kim was completely into it, she stepped back slowly keeping her nipple in Ty's mouth and laid across the bench.

Ty got down on his knees on the side of the bench and continued to suck on her nipples. Kim spread her legs open, leaning one of them over the rail. She started touching herself and her vagina was dripping wet. She moved her fingers in a circular motion over her clit while Ty sucked on her nipple. She loved every bit of it and she wanted him inside of her, badly.

Ty watched Kim as she touched herself and enjoyed it. She almost looked as if she was going to cum. Ty popped Kim's hand and stopped her from touching herself.

"It's my job to make her cum," he said seductively.

He ripped her panties off and tapped her pussy. He moved his fingers in the same motion Kim was. She spread her legs wider now, letting him know she wanted him where he was. He kept moving his fingers around as he took his other hand and slipped his middle finger inside her pussy. This made Kim let out a little moan.

Ty was turned on more now. He kept his finger going in and out of Kim while still rubbing her clit with his others. Each time he pushed his finger inside her, he moved the tip of his finger in a "come here" motion.

Each time he did this he was hitting Kim's G spot. She was gyrating her waist in a circular motion on his finger, enjoying it. She started moaning even louder now.

"I'm about to cum, I'm *about to um…*" she let out in a slutty voice.

Ty watched his fingers turn creamy as he kept thrusting them inside of Kim. He placed his mouth on her vagina and sucked her clit while she came.

"AHHHHH!" Kim moaned almost louder than the music.

Ty kept sucking until she finished and dropped her legs. He grabbed her limp body and turned her around on her stomach. He lifted her by her waist, positioning her on all fours and wasted no time ramming his dick inside of Kim's pussy. He was rock hard and ready.

Kim's insides were tight, wet, and warm. Ty moaned each time her walls gripped his shaft. He started pounding himself into her as he held her waist and she arched her back. She wanted him inside of her just as much as he wanted to be there. She placed her arms down and leaned on her elbows as she started to throw her ass back. She twerked, jerked and bounced all on his dick while throwing it back on each stroke. They were breathing heavily, moaning and enjoying themselves.

"Can I cum on daddy's dick?" Kim asked Ty in a baby voice.

"I can't hear you, speak up," Ty answered as he gave her a harder stroke.

Kim let out a moan, "Can I cum on daddy's dick?" she asked again, almost yelling now.

"Say please," Ty told her as he stroked harder and harder.

"Please, can I cum on daddyy's dickkk?" Kim drug her words out as her body began to tingle and vibrate. She felt like she was about to burst, and each stroke of Ty's was hitting the right spot.

She screamed as her body slowly released one of the greatest feelings ever. She moaned and shook while her vagina emptied itself onto Ty's bare dick. He kept stroking, watching the cum ooze out on his penis. *It's my turn now*, he thought to himself as he pushed Kim completely on her stomach.

"Put ya fuckin' ass up," he told her as he slapped her ass cheek. She did as she was told and arched her back putting her ass in the air.

Ty admired looking at her plump pussy from this angle. He rammed himself back into Kim and pounded until he came. He left every drip of his cum inside of her. It felt too good for him to pull out.

Out of breath now, he sat down on the end of the couch, enjoying the breeze of fresh air. Kim was still laid out flat on her stomach, panting and trying to relax. She felt amazing and she could fall asleep right where she was. Ty stood up and grabbed her by her arm.

"Let's go," he told her as he walked her back inside of the room into the bedroom.

He pulled the sheets and cover back, and then tapped on the plush bed for Kim to get in. She admired everything about their night. She jumped in the bed with no problem and admired Ty as he climbed in. She turned on her side and he pulled her close to him wrapping his arms around her. They both fell sound asleep.

The next morning Kim woke up to a lonely bed. Ty was gone. She looked over at the clock and saw it was 11:30 am; check out was in a half hour. She jumped up immediately to check the closet for her money. She opened her duffle bag and counted her straps of money. It was all there. She took a deep breath as she thought about the wild night her and Ty had, she couldn't wait to tell Toya. She picked her dress up and threw it back on, put on her coat and grabbed her shoes. She left the room feeling amazing.

Kim drove straight to Toya's place and let herself in. Toya was laying in her bed watching TV when Kim busted in and jumped on her.

"What the hell?" Toya laughed as she pushed her friend off of her. "I guess you got some dick last night, huh?" she joked.

"Girl I got more than dick bitch. I'm pregnant," Kim and Toya busted out laughing. They always made jokes about their sex life. "No for real though, I do have to go get a plan b. No, we didn't use protection and *don't* judge me. That nigga fucked the shit out of me girl! He's a freak, just how I like them. I'm keeping his ass around," Kim laughed as she meant what she told her friend. After one encounter she was hooked.

"I don't know about this Kim. You sure you can mix business and pleasure? You know how that shit goes." Toya was fine with whatever decision her friend made but she had to voice her opinion.

"Don't worry T, I ain't gonna get crazy," Kim laughed. "I'm not looking for love right now anyway, but he has some *bomb ass* D and I love his energy. We ain't gone be able to see each other all the time anyway. He's gone be like my once or twice a month boo thang," she told her friend. Toya was cool with it. She always had her back no matter what and never judged her.

"Now come on," Kim told Toya, "Let's go get this pill and some lunch. Its damn near 3 and I haven't eaten all day. And oh yeah, shopping cause we got paid today," Kim smiled as she thought about the money in her trunk. Her and Toya headed out the door into the Brooklyn streets.

Kim opened her eyes. She was falling asleep, deep in her thoughts. She tried to wiggle her wrist around and she couldn't. The rope that tied her hands down to the chair was wrapped too tight. She started to cry as she realized she was helpless. *Why, why, why*, she thought to herself as she started to feel sorry.

"Shut that crying shit up," Kim was talking to herself out loud. "Look at you, crying and ready to give up. Suck that shit up," she continued. *But it's over for me. I can't do anything now* she answered herself in her head. "It's not over until you stop breathing, as long as you have breath in your body, you know you're still here for a reason. After all the shit you've been through Kim, you're telling me you're giving up? I thought I'd never see the day," Kim was speaking out loud again. *You're a stupid little girl, how dare you cry and ask why after all of the lives you took. You deserve everything you're going through.* A third voice in her head was speaking.

She knew she was on the verge of breaking down. Her bipolar disorder was triggering and she felt it. "SHUT UP!" she yelled out loud. She was speaking to all of the voices in her head. She wanted it to stop, "I'm going to get myself out of this shit and that's it! You bitches shut up!" She told herself. She couldn't let her thoughts take over. She had to stay strong and sane. Her mind drifted to Toya. She missed her friend dearly and now she felt like she was close to seeing her again. She wished she could rewind time, but she knew she couldn't.

Suddenly, Kim heard a door open. She looked up and saw a figure but couldn't see clear enough. From the body shape of the figure could tell that it was a man or a rather large woman. The person walked up to her with what looked like a towel in their hand.

"What are you doing?" Kim asked as they came closer and closer to her.

The person was standing behind her now and Kim couldn't see what they were doing. "What the fuck are you doing?" Kim asked again this time screaming nervously.

The mystery man placed the towel over her face which contained Chloroform and she fell asleep instantly...

CHAPTER TEN

Q woke up shaking and drenched in sweat. It was the day he had to lay Toya to rest and he had no idea how he was going to do it. He had been suffering since her death in the worse way, especially now knowing what her and Kim were really up to. *Kim*, he thought to himself. He didn't want to think about her right now. What he told Frankie to do was killing his soul but he knew it had to be done.

He turned and looked at his alarm clock. It was 7:08 a.m. and Toya's funeral started at 10. He wanted to be at Momma Margaret's by 9, so he had to get up now. He took a deep breath, stretched, then got up out of his bed. Momma insisted that everyone wore yellow and white and that the immediate family wore all white. Q had on an all-white suit with yellow cuff links. He still wanted to wear Toya's favorite color.

He closed his eyes thinking about how he had to sit right next to Momma, knowing he was the reason they were burying her daughter. He felt sick. He thought he was wrong at first for making Kim miss her funeral, but he wanted everyone to feel how he felt, inconsolable. He grabbed his towel and washcloth and headed to the shower.

As the water ran over his chest, he couldn't help but think about how he drugged Kim last night and fucked her in all those crazy ways. It was mind boggling to Q how all of this shit unfolded. He never imagined his first time fucking Kim again would be the way that it was. Shit, he never imagined the two turning on him. He shook these thoughts out of his head and finished his shower.

Kim awoke again in the same place, tied to the same chair. Her memory was still hazy, and she still had no idea what was going on. She was certain that it was the next day now and the day of Toya's funeral and she was still kidnapped. It killed her that she still had no idea if Q was alright or not.

"Good morning," Kim heard a voice that brought her back to where she was, but she couldn't answer. "I said good morning bitch," the voice said again. It took Kim a minute to answer; she was trying to figure out who this man was.

"Who the fuck are you?" Kim answered the voice. Frankie back-slapped Kim and blood flew from her mouth

"I ask the questions not you. Now let's try again, good morning," Frankie was rubbing the side of Kim's face with his hand.

"Fuck you!" Kim said and then spit in his face.

"Wrong answer," Frankie said as he slapped Kim again and then punched her in the stomach. Kim started coughing and screamed out, "bastard." Frankie started laughing and walking around Kim in a circle. "You're a tough little cookie huh," he said, walking as he was talking. "I guess you wanna be here all day, that's fine with me," Frankie walked away and disappeared into the darkness.

Q was dressed to impress and ready to go. It was 8:40 a.m. now and he had 20 mins to get to Mommas. He looked at himself one more time in the mirror before heading out the door. The crisp white suit looked great on his smooth chocolate skin and the yellow bow tie highlighted it. His beard was neatly brushed and his shape up was fresh. His curls had an extra shine to them. He wanted to look perfect for Toya. He grabbed his shades and left.

Q drove through Brooklyn playing "Tony Story" by Meek Mills and he couldn't help but think how he had so many snakes around him. He had to get to the bottom of this fucked up situation. He turned his music down as he pulled up to Mommas, double parked in front of her building, he went inside to get her. He heard Momma crying when he walked in and he took a deep breath. He had to hold it together for her today.

"Hey Momma, I'm here," he walked in her room and gave her a hug.

"Oh hey baby," Momma said as she hugged Q back, trying to hide the cry in her voice. "You look so handsome, look at my boy," she said as she stepped back to get a full view of Q. He smiled. He loved Momma Margaret so much. She still found a way to make him smile with all the pain in her heart. She was a beautiful woman.

"And look at you momma, looking like fine wine," Q said as they both giggled.

The room felt a little warm. For a second there was a little joy around. Momma grabbed her coat and they both headed out the door to pay their final respects to Toya.

It was 9:20 now. Q and Momma had made it to the church. They were the first ones there besides the pastor. The church looked beautiful with flowers everywhere. So many people had sent their condolences in the form of flowers that you could tell Toya was truly loved. There were poster boards all around Toya's casket with pictures of her throughout life. Q stared at the pictures taking it all in. It was real, his sister was gone, and this was his final goodbye.

He walked over to Momma who was standing over Toya's beautiful white casket rocking back and forth and he placed his arm over her. "It's okay Momma, it's gonna be ok," he told her, lying to himself knowing it would never be okay. Momma didn't speak. Q left her alone and went to greet people at the door as they started to arrive.

About forty-five minutes had passed since Kim was left in the dark by this unnamed stranger. She'd been screaming for what felt like hours for help and no one came. She broke down crying. She just knew it was over for her. She couldn't believe she was missing her best friend's funeral and she had no idea if Q was safe or not.

She screamed in anger, "you mother fuckers, fuck you." Then suddenly she heard footsteps. She tried her best to get herself together without being able to use her body parts.

"Did you ring?" Frankie asked sarcastically. Kim didn't say a word, she didn't want him to leave her alone again, so she thought maybe she'd just listen this time. "What's wrong little lady, the cat's got your tongue?" Frankie laughed, still being sarcastic.

"What do you want from me?" Kim asked with hostility in her voice.

Frankie became serious, he moved his face close enough to Kim's to almost kiss her. "I wanna know who gave you and your friend the drop on that last robbery y'all committed."

Kim became nervous and her arms filled with goosebumps. *Oh shit! This can't be Ty's people! Someone's tryna get at Ty*, she thought to herself. Kim was extra confused now and it took a second for her to answer.

"I don't know what you're talking about," Kim lied.

Frankie hit Kim twice again in her face, "you're a liar and I'll beat you until you tell the truth." He meant what he said.

"You know what I hate about pretty females like you Kim," Frankie started speaking. Kim was trying to figure out how he knew her name, but it was obvious he did his homework before coming for her. "Y'all are grimy, y'all are low key, low key devils. My boss has been more than loyal to me, more than loyal to the people around him, and I have so much love and respect for him. I've never seen him disrespect a female for as long as I've known him. He's an all-around, great guy. Which is why I'm so confused as to why you and your friend were snaking him. And even more confused as to why you want to protect the man responsible," Frankie wasn't finished with his lecture, but Kim was confused.

"I don't know what the fuck you're talking about okay. I don't know who your boss is. *You* might have the wrong girl," Kim was telling the truth this time. She thought she was being held by Ty's people for the way the last robbery ended, but now she had no idea what was going on.

"And you bitches love lying, another thing I hate," Frankie continued. "You know who my boss is, and he knows you very well. In fact, he knows you so well that he couldn't believe you were the one robbing him. That's where I come in. I'm going to get to the bottom of this, whether you cooperate or not," he said with conviction.

Frankie meant his words. Kim was bewildered. *Who the hell is his boss that knows me well?* she thought to herself. She couldn't figure it out. She thought and thought and she couldn't put it together. *Who would be after Ty? Who is this boss guy?* She had no answers.

Frankie pulled out a gun and put it in Kim's mouth, "I have orders to blow your head off whether you tell me or not but especially if you don't."

Frankie looked Kim directly in the eye while he spoke. Kim wasn't ready to die, especially not for Ty, but damn, was she gonna snitch? She tried to think fast. She knew now the hit out on Toya didn't come from Ty's people, so it was harder now for her to give him up. *Fuck that, I wanna live.*

She tried to speak with the gun in her mouth the best she could, "uhkay uhkay."

Frankie removed the gun slowly. "Are we ready to talk?" Frankie asked with the gun still close enough to slide it right back in her mouth. Kim nodded her head yes. "I don't understand that, speak up bitch!" Frankie was so disrespectful.

"Yes, I'm ready to talk," Kim was angry, hurt, and embarrassed. She knew that if she wasn't taken advantage of, she would have had a better chance to defend herself. "I work for Ty," she whispered.

"What? Speak up," Frankie replied. He didn't hear her.

"I work for, well I *was* working for a guy named Ty. He's from out of town. I don't think you would know him." Kim felt so low after giving up his name, but she had to save herself. Ty was no good anyway. He was probably still after her. It just so happened these motherfuckers caught her first.

Frankie's eyes lit up; he knew Ty. He handled all the drop offs for Q. Him and his boys did most of the dirty work. Frankie couldn't believe it. He looked at Kim with disgust and said, "You a grimy bitch!" Before she could respond, Frankie butted her with the gun and knocked her out.

"Why should I feel discouraged,

why should the shadows come.

Why should my heart feel lonely,

and long for heaven and home.

When Jesus is my portion,

a constant friend is He.

His eye is on the sparrow,

and I know he watches over me.

His eye is on the sparrow,

and I know he watches me."

One of Toya's cousins with a beautiful voice was singing "His Eye Is On The Sparrow" by Lauryn Hill and Tanya Blount. Her voice was touching Q's heart and he really didn't listen to too much "church music" as he would call it. Momma Margaret was sitting next to Q with a blank look on her face. She was slowly rocking back and forth as tears were silently falling from her eyes.

Q had so many mixed emotions. He didn't know what to do. He didn't know if he could sit through the funeral any longer. He wanted to get up and leave, but he knew he had to be here for Momma Margaret and he had to speak. He took a deep breath and looked around.

The church was packed out. Seats were full and people were standing in the doorways. Toya was loved by so many. All Q saw when he looked around was crying faces, he felt so guilty.

> *"I sing because I'm happy,*
>
> *I sing because I'm free.*
>
> *His eye is on the sparrow.*
>
> *And I know He watches me, He watches me,*
>
> *His eye is on the sparrow*
>
> *and I know He watches, I know He watches,*
>
> *I know He watches me"*

The beautiful voice filled the church with more cries as she sang. Momma Margaret was standing now and raising her hand in the air. Q stood up with her, rubbing her back while she let her cries out.

His phone started going off in his pocket. He knew that the only person who would be calling him right now was Frankie. His mind went to Kim. He didn't even know how to feel about the situation anymore. He didn't answer his phone. He told Frankie if he missed the call to just shoot him a text. Sure enough, like clockwork, Frankie sent Q a text saying *Ty.*

Q was shocked. Ty was the motherfucking snake. Q and Ty had been boys for years before they became partners in doing business. Now they were getting money together and Ty was one of the closest people to Q. He handled all business being brought in and sent out. He lived in Long Island and Q tried to keep him a distance away from his family. Since Q was close to him, he was really only around for celebrations. He never came across as disloyal to Q and they only ever had one fake issue. Ty wanted Q to put one of his cousins on that had recently came home from jail at the time, but Q wasn't with it. He didn't like doing business with anyone he didn't know or anyone who didn't come well recommended. He trusted Ty but he didn't know his cousin from a whole in the wall and he refused to have any parts of him.

Ty took no for an answer well Q thought, *there's no way that's the reason he could have done this.* Q started thinking. There was one-time Ty saw Kim and Q had to tell him that she was off limits but again, Q didn't feel like that could be a reason for him to do what he had done. *Was he just jealous? What the fuck was it?* Q thought to himself thoroughly.

He texted Frankie back and said *well done, keep on with the plan.* Q brought his focus back to the funeral and Momma Margaret. She was still standing, this time she had both of her hands up and she was hunched over crying hard. Q continued to rub her back and stood there feeling vile.

When the soloist was finished, the preacher called on the people who wanted to share a few words. Q walked up with sweaty palms as he was about to speak in front of so many people. He took a deep breath and took his time getting himself together.

"Good morning everyone," Q began to speak. "I'm not really good at speeches, but I just want to say a few things," Q tugged on his bow tie nervously.

"Take ya time baby," an older voice yelled out from the crowd.

Q took a deep breath again and spoke, "Toya was a beautiful person. I met her over 20 years ago and we have been great, great friends ever since. She was my best friend." Q put his head down he couldn't stop the tears from falling.

He took another deep breath and started again, "If she was with you, then she was with you. There was no questioning her loyalty. People like that are hard to find these days, *real friends* are hard to find these days. Genuine, loving, and caring people are hard to find these days and I found all of that in my friend. Now it's going to be almost impossible to live without her."

Q had everyone in their feelings. People were yelling out "its ok" and "amen" and "poor son." His words were touching.

"I wrote my sister a poem." he continued. "Dear Toya, you were so beautiful. I know heaven is shining. You were so loved. It hurts that it shows with you dying.

Look at all the people that came out to see you. I know God makes no mistakes and he will keep you. Save a spot for me up there, cause now it's too lonely down here. I'll give anything to see you smile again. I'll forever love you best friend. Rest easy T," Q walked away from the mic. He was angry. He couldn't even go sit back down next to Momma. He kept walking and went outside.

Everyone was clapping, crying, and saying how beautiful his words were. Q didn't want to hear that. He meant every word, but it still didn't change the fact that he caused this. He had to get his hands on Ty. It was killing him that all this shit was happening. He stayed outside for a while to get his mind right. He didn't want to go back into the church. It it was too depressing, but of course he had no choice.

He went back in and it was time to view the body. He didn't want to see her like that, so he stayed seated. So many people stopped over Toya's casket while walking pass to say something, to kiss her, and to just simply stare and probably replay memories in their head. Momma Margaret stayed seated also, Q figured she wasn't ready either.

"That was a beautiful speech Q. You know Toya loves you and I know she's looking down on you right now proud," Momma was still trying to comfort Q even with her own broken heart.

"Thank you, Momma," was all Q could say.

Was she proud or was she mad as hell at me right now? Why did y'all have to be into this fuckin shit T? Q thought to himself. He couldn't shake this shit.

After everyone finally finished saying their goodbyes to Toya, the preacher gave the directions to the cemetery where Toya would be buried. Everyone was leaving out and Momma Margaret stayed behind. She walked up to the casket and put her hand on Toya's face. She kissed her on her cheek.

"Why God why? Why my baby? My only baby," Momma Margaret broke down.

Q couldn't handle it anymore. He was trying his best to be there for Momma, but the thoughts and emotions were eating him alive. He contemplated walking out, but he couldn't leave her like this. He walked over to the casket and started rubbing Mommas back.

"It's okay Momma, I know my words won't fix anything but I'm here for you," he meant what he said.

"Oh Q, you don't understand. I can't leave this church without my baby! I'm not leaving this church without my baby! I'm not putting my baby in that ground. Come on Q, help me get her *home*! Help me take my baby home where she belongs!" Momma began crying harder and harder. Q was in disbelief. Momma was losing herself. He grabbed her and hugged her tight.

"She's where she belongs now Momma. She's home. She's in heaven, she's an angel, she's watching over us now." Q kept hugging Momma.

"I don't wanna hear that Q! I'm where she belongs! She belongs with *me*! Oh god, why'd you take my baby? You should've taken me with her," Momma kept crying.

Q's words weren't working. He had to get momma home. He didn't think she would be able to handle the burial. He asked the preacher to hold off on the burial until he was able to get back. He had to take care of Momma Margaret before she passed out.

Momma refused to go home. Q couldn't get through to her. She said she would get herself together in the limo. He helped her walk out of the church and to the back of the limo. He closed the door after she got in and tapped the back of the car to let the driver know he could pull off. He told Momma he would meet them there.

Q called Frankie back. "Yes boss," he answered on the second ring.

"How's it going?" Q asked.

"As planned boss. She's still out cold," Frankie responded.

"Okay, bring her to me at the meeting spot," Q said before hanging up the phone. He jumped in his car and headed to meet Frankie. He felt fucked up about Kim missing the funeral so he was going to bring her to the burial. She had some explaining to do anyway.

Kim woke up with a pounding headache in the back of what looked like a limo. Her body was in so much pain and her face felt swollen. When she gathered herself, she realized she was locked in the backseat of the limo. The doors must have been on safety lock and the glass divider between the back and driver seat was closed.

What the fuck is going on now, Kim thought to herself. She looked out the window and realized she was in a cemetery. A few seconds later, she realized there was a burial going on. *Oh my God*! *Is this Toya's funeral*?

Kim became hot, she couldn't believe whoever had her was putting her through this much torture. She wanted to get out of the limo and see her friend's casket, she already missed her chance to see her and rub her face one last time. She wanted to kiss her, pray over a rose, and let it go in the ground with her.

From where the limo was parked, she couldn't see well enough to point people out, but she was more than sure it was for Toya. *I love you so much Toya baby! I swear to God himself I do! Save me a spot baby!*

A tear fell from Kim's swollen eyes. Everything was happening too fast for her, from waking up kidnapped, being pregnant and beat, to now waking up, locked in a car at her best friend's burial whose funeral she missed. *What would Momma Margaret think? I was supposed to be right there with her during this.* Kim's thoughts were all over. She was angry and she felt so helpless. She hated the fact that she was caught off guard and couldn't defend herself. She just watched out the window and cried as her thoughts went haywire.

Q dropped his flower on Toya's casket. *This is the end now,* he thought to himself. He couldn't see her again and he'd have to come talk to the ground to be the closest to her. He stepped back and closed his eyes, "I love you T," he said and then blew a kiss before opening his eyes.

He sat back down in his seat and watched how everyone else dropped their flowers and then started to depart. So many people were hurt, Q could see it all in their faces, even with the ones who wore glasses. He could see the tear stains on their cheeks.

It took time before everyone walked off, leaving just Momma and Q. Momma was drained. Q could see there was little life left in her and he felt awful. She was going home to an empty house and the only person she shared it with for so long was gone, her only daughter. Q shook his head. He wondered when it would get easier for him or if it was going to be this hard forever.

Momma was ready to go. Q offered to walk her to her car, but she refused. She told him he'd done enough and thanked him from the bottom of her heart. She needed to be alone now. She took her time as she left the grave site. It seemed like she was dreading this goodbye. Q waited for momma to get in the car and for the driver to pull off before he called Frankie and told him to bring Kim out. He was more than ready to get to the bottom of this shit.

Kim watched as someone started walking towards the limo. She decided to play sleep. She thought that maybe they would say something around her that could help her figure this out. Instead, they opened the door and shook her to wake up.

"Let's go sleeping snake," Frankie said in a disgusted voice.

Kim was tired of this nigga and his disrespect. She wanted to kick his face in, but she stayed calm. She didn't have the strength anyway. He grabbed her by her arm and started walking her towards the burial she was watching through the window. *Where the hell is he taking me*? Kim thought to herself. She kept walking.

As they became closer, she saw that there was someone sitting under the tent. She was confused but she had no choice but to keep walking. Frankie sat her down in a chair directly behind the person that was already sitting there. She sat down as she was told and looked over at the casket. It was beautiful. It had what looked like a quilt with a picture of Toya airbrushed on it covering the whole casket. The picture was beautiful. Toya was smiling so bright and she had angel wings added behind her with white and yellow doves in the sky. The words "Rest In Peace T" were written beautifully in script under her picture.

"How could you do this shit to me Kim," Q finally spoke. Kim's heart stopped

"Q?!" she yelled and jumped up to walk in front of him. "Q, what the fuck! You did this shit to me?!" Kim was hurt and confused.

Q saw her face and felt fucked up. She was still so pretty with her bruises. He couldn't believe she was trying to play victim.

"Bitch, you did this shit to me! Look where the fuck we at Kim. Toya's dead because of me." Q started crying. He couldn't keep his shield on around Kim. She was the person who saw his soul on the inside.

Kim was crying. She didn't even know why; she was just crying. Too much was going on. She was finally around the one person she thought she was safe with and he was the one causing the pain.

"Q, what the fuck are you talking about? You're confusing me. How did you kill Toya? What do you mean?" she asked him while still crying.

"Kim, *STOP FUCKING PLAYING WITH ME!*" Q was getting angry now, "*YOU KNOW WHAT THE FUCK IS GOING ON BITCH! YOU WAS ROBBING ME WITH TY!*"

Kim never heard Q speak to her this way. She could tell he wasn't playing at all.

"Ty? What! You know Ty? Q, I worked for him for a few months. I didn't know you knew that nigga! I swear to God I didn't know! Oh my god… So you sent the hit to Toya? Damn Q, I'm so sorry, I swear to *God on my life* baby, I did not know." Kim felt horrible. She honestly had no idea that Ty and Q were connected.

Q wanted to believe her so bad. He knew that there was a possibility that she didn't know, but Toya was already gone so somebody had to pay for their mistakes. Q didn't say a word and Kim continued to try and convince him of the truth.

"Q I swear! You've gotta believe me. I was going to come to you and tell you everything. I needed you to help me get the niggas that did this shit to Toya. I feel fucked up over this shit. It's just as much my fault as it is anyone else's. Toya didn't even wanna do this shit... I forced her," Kim said, crying harder now. "This shit wasn't supposed to go this far. We started out only drugging rich, old, white pigs before we met Ty. I swear to you Q, I never knew we was hitting you. He never gave us any information about the people we were robbing. He set it up and we just followed his rules."

Kim looked Q dead in his eyes as she said this. He knew Kim, he knew when she lied, and he knew when she told the truth. Right now, everything was telling him that she was telling the truth. It fucked him up because he wanted to believe her but he didn't know if it was only because she was scared now. Kim was his bitch and Toya was his sister. He never had to question their loyalty before. They both were in his heart and he would never have thought they'd move like this; he believed Kim.

"Kim," Q started to speak, "if my heart is right, then I believe you. It fucked me up to even think that you had something to do with this shit, but I didn't understand it. I knew how close you and Toya were. I felt like you had to know something about her death because the shit ain't make no sense. I got my own shit going on, I do my own type of operation, that *I* tried to keep away from y'all. I never wanted my family to get caught up in my bullshit cause niggas get grimy. Then, I find out in the most fucked up way that my bitch and my sister were doing their own thing too. They so low that they bumping into my niggas. Ty was my right-hand man. I can't believe this shit."

Q looked at Kim. Her lips were swollen and one of her eyes were black. He felt bad he made Frankie put his hands on her. Now he thought about hurting Frankie the same way he did Rico. *Frankie was only being loyal to me*, Q thought. It would be wrong of him to kill him for that. He still thought about it.

Kim interrupted his thoughts, "Q, let's get this nigga. He played the both of us. You know me, you know T. This shit is our word against his. We gotta get this nigga outta here."

Kim meant every word. She started thinking about the baby. She didn't know if she should tell Q now about it or not, but she felt like she needed to go to the hospital. She was bleeding and she thought it was from Frankie hitting her in her stomach. She didn't want to hold anymore secrets from Q, so she decided to tell him.

"Q, there's more," Kim started, now placing her hands on top of her head. "I started fucking with Ty and I slipped up. Now I'm pregnant."

Q looked at Kim disgusted. *Now she was fucking this nigga too*!? Q started thinking about how Ty wanted Kim before. Now he started to take this shit real personal. Q felt stupid that he didn't realize this beforehand. He didn't think that little issue was enough to make his homie turn on him. *I guess jealousy could make you do some foul shit*, Q thought. He couldn't hate Kim, she was used in this situation but even her line of work was grimy. *Everybody got their own demons*, Q thought, *at least I know she wouldn't purposely put them on me.*

It took everything in Q to put all of this behind him. He grabbed Kim and hugged her tight. He squeezed her as she cried in his arms. For a second Q felt complete. He got to the bottom of the situation and even though he was responsible for Toya's death, everyone held themselves accountable. Losing Toya was bringing them closer.

"Go ahead and say goodbye," Q told Kim pointing at Toya's casket. He handed her a rose. She walked to Toya's casket and closed her eyes as she said her last words.

"I love you so much Toya, you already know what's up. I'm sorry you had to go by yourself baby but save us a spot so when we get there, we'll turn it up," she kissed her rose and placed it on the casket. She kissed the tip of her fingers and touched the casket. She walked back over to Q and he put his arm around her shoulder. They both turned around and walked towards Q's limo.

CHAPTER ELEVEN

Back home now, Q had to figure out a way to get to Ty. He knew it wouldn't be that easy because he lived out of town. *I could reschedule the drop*, he thought to himself. Ty was scheduled to make a drop off next week and Q thought he could tell him it's been moved up sooner.

He decided to call him, "What's up Q baby?" Ty said in a regular way. Usually, Q would be cool to hear this but knowing what he knew now, he despised hearing his voice.

"Yo, the ice cream company called. They said instead of delivering the chocolate next week, they wanna bring it tonight. They said they are over-booked, and tonight would be better," Q said, speaking in codes.

He always heard about dealers getting caught up from talking too much on the phone. He was referring to his dope.

"Oh word? Aight, aight, that's even better for me. I'll see em' at the same spot and time," Ty answered.

Q hung up. He had to plan for the night because he knew it was going to get ugly.

Ty hung up the phone. He already knew what time it was. He hated the fact that Q thought he was a dummy. As long as they've been in business, Q has never made a move like this. If the connect was to ever try to reschedule anything, Q wouldn't trust it. He knew something was up.

Ty started thinking about how all this shit was getting crazy. When he sent his boys to merk Toya and Kim, thinking they would be together, he saw someone else had already started with Toya. He knew Q had to know something. He had stressed to them both how important it was to never leave any witnesses. They fucked up big time on their last run. He thought maybe he could wait it out and Q would take care of Kim too. He didn't expect Q to find out he was involved and now that he received this call, he knew it was gonna go down. He was going to meet Q but he wasn't going to meet him alone. He called his two hittas, Lance and Nate. They were always ready for action and Nate already felt a way towards Q.

"Yo, I need something cleaned up tonight. Be ready by 6," Ty said as he hung up. He started thinking about Q and how it was all about to go down tonight. He was finally getting the chance to get rid of him.

Ty started feeling a way about Q once he felt like he started to let the money get to him. In all reality, Ty was just jealous. He remembered the first time he'd saw Kim. They were all out celebrating. Him and Q were in the cut of the club so they could see everything that was going on. They never wanted to be caught off guard no matter where they were. He saw Kim when she walked in and she was fine as hell. She was light skinned with chinky eyes and full lips. Ty had a weak spot for pretty red bones and she had an ass on her. Toya was right behind her highlighting her beauty. She was just as fine in a darker color.

"Yo, who is that right there? I need her," Ty asked Q while pointing at Kim.

"Oh yeah, you need her?" Q let out a little laugh. "Well need on, cause that's me right there. And the one behind her is my sister, both fine and off limits," Q told him in a serious tone.

Ty didn't like the way Q told him this. "Man, how that's ya bitch and you here with Monica? You trippin' nigga, you gotta share," Ty laughed but he wasn't joking.

"I don't give a fuck who I'm here with nigga. These is my hoes. That's my bitch and she's off limits to my niggas, that's all I'm saying. It's a million other females in here, pick another one." Q did not like to repeat himself about shit that he meant the first time he said it. He had a bit of an attitude when he was speaking.

Ty felt it. He didn't like the fact that Q thought he could just tell him what he could or couldn't do. *Niggas' bitches get fucked every day Q, you'll be aight.* Ty thought to himself as he planned to definitely get next to Kim. He chilled for a little while then left the club before everyone else. This was the second time Q rubbed him the wrong way and he wasn't feeling his vibe.

The first time was when he didn't wanna put his cousin Nate on when he first came out of prison and was fucked up. He wasn't worried about his cousin because he knew he could do his own thing eventually, but the fact that Q could have helped it happen quicker, Ty already worked for him, and Q wouldn't put him on, didn't sit well with him. This Kim situation was the last straw, Ty didn't believe in three strikes.

For a long time, he tried so hard to figure out how he was going to get next to Kim without it being in Q's face. When he ran in to Kim at one of his drops, he thought it was the devil himself allowing his devilish ways to come out. The only reason Kim and Toya didn't die that day was because of who Kim was. He wanted her at the club the first time he saw her, and he had to have her once he saw what she was about at the hotel. She turned the bad in him on. It was quicker than expected when Kim finally gave him some pussy and it was everything and more. He saw why Q was the way he was over her now. Ty came back to his thoughts. He looked at his watch for the time and got ready for his night.

Q called Frankie to tell him the plan. He went into the bathroom so he wouldn't wake Kim from sleeping. He had just brought her home from his private doctor, Dr. Z, and she was having a miscarriage. He felt horrible about the things she went through and he knew she needed her rest.

"What's up boss?" Frankie answered on the first ring.

"I'm handling that business with Ty tonight. I need you to be ready," Q said.

"You know I'm always ready boss," Frankie was a man of his word. This was another reason Q knew he couldn't be mad at him over Kim.

"I'm meeting him at the Cloverdale Warehouse at 8," he told Frankie.

"Aight," was all Frankie said.

Q hung up his phone and walked out of the bathroom. He looked over at Kim and saw she was still fast asleep. He wanted to kiss her swollen face and rub her body but he had work to do. He changed his clothes, grabbed his duffle bag from the closet and slipped out the door.

Kim was pretending to be asleep. She overheard Q's conversation and now she wanted to be there. She wanted to kill Ty just as much as Q and she had some anger to let out. She didn't feel right, lying in bed knowing what was about to go down. She had to move and move quick.

The first thing she was going to do was go to her apartment and get her things. Up and out of bed now, she was putting her clothes and shoes on. She grabbed her cell phone, keys, and headed out the door. She stood on the corner for about three minutes, flagging a cabbie down. It took her about 15 minutes to get to her place from Q's. When she got to her door, she took a deep breath before turning the knob. She hadn't been home since Toya died and her place held so many memories. It was like they shared homes. Walking into her own home felt like a stranger's. Kim remembered the days when walking into her place felt like everything. With Toya missing now, nothing felt the same. She was incomplete and missing her friend badly. The food in her kitchen was spoiled, the furniture was dusty and her plants were dried out. Kim had no desire to water them. She grabbed her small bamboo plant that Toya had recently gifted her.

She went to her closet first and moved the shoe boxes that were covering her safe. She unlocked it and checked for her money as if it could've been missing. She loved to double check just in case. She counted it and surely it was all there.

The next thing she checked for was her passport and the keys to her back up spot. The more money she made messing with Ty, the smarter she became. She had a secret house she was paying off just in case she ever had to disappear. Kim knew after this shit went down with Ty tonight, her and Q were going to have to get low. She wanted to be well prepared. She packed a duffle bag with enough belongings for about a week or two. Anything needed beyond that would be bought she thought. She had enough money to be comfortable for a while. Her and Toya had some savings. After working for Ty, they were able to afford more things than before. *Toya's money, I could give it to Momma,* she decided. She just had to figure out a way to give it to her without telling her it was dirty money. She would think about that later she thought, right now she had to get ready to leave.

As she went through her belongings in her room, she couldn't help but to think about Toya. They had so much fun together between here and Toya's place. They were so excited and scared at the same time when they moved out on their own. Some nights they stayed together at Kim's and others at Toya's until they were comfortable enough to stay alone. They never invited any men over to their place that they were dealing with. That was always a major no-no for them, only family was allowed at home.

Kim went to her jewelry box and started going through it. She put on a chain that Toya had recently bought her for her birthday. It was the half of a heart that said sisters forever. Toya had the other half. Kim wanted her to be buried with it on but being kidnapped ruined that plan. She kissed the chain after putting it on; she missed her friend so much. She put all of her jewelry into a Ziplock bag and put it in her duffle bag.

Kim walked over to her nightstand and checked her draws for anything she might have overlooked. She found an old picture of her and Q. It looked like they were out at Coney Island. They always had so much fun together. She grabbed the picture and put it in her duffle bag. This made her go to her living room and grab her photo albums. She was taking more than she expected and she had to hurry up. Now she wished she had more time. In case she wasn't able to come back, she didn't want to leave behind anything important to her.

Suddenly she remembered she paid her rent up for 6 months last month. She started thinking maybe she could come back or somehow arrange for her stuff to be put in storage. *I'll figure this out later*, she thought.

She grabbed everything she had and headed to the parking garage to get her car. She put all of her belongings in the trunk and sat in the driver's seat thinking. Q had no idea that she was going to meet up with him and Ty. She was ready, but she wished she had someone to go with her. Whenever she had to do anything, she always had Toya right there with her.

She took a deep breath. There was something she had forgotten. Kim ran back inside of her apartment and went to her closet. She changed into an all-black sweat suit and a pair of black Timbs. She put her long hair into a ponytail and put on a baseball cap. She tucked her chain under her shirt. Now she was ready for action.

She pulled her black BMW out of the garage and was headed to the freeway. She looked at her dashboard and saw that she had a full tank of gas. She was going to need it. The Cloverdale Warehouse was a few hours away. She wanted to get there before everyone. She didn't have a plan yet, but she had enough driving time to figure it out. She drove down Brooklyn's streets playing Al bee Al, one of her favorite rappers.

"Now, I don't know what this nigga Q got planned, but I know something is up," Ty was talking to Lance and Nate. "He might be on some man-to-man shit, but he might also have niggas waiting, I don't know. I do know I wanna handle that motherfucker myself," Ty said, speaking with hatred in his voice as he held his gun in his hand admiring it. He knew what type of man Q was so he knew he probably would want it to be them both, but he had to be ready just in case.

"Man, fuck that nigga! Let's just shoot his ass up," Nate said. He didn't like Q only because he didn't want to look out for him when he got out of jail. He was from the hood just like Q. He felt like Q thought he was better than them.

Ty thought about what Nate said, *they could just walk in and start blazing.* He wasn't sure how it was going to happen, but he was ready for whatever it was.

"Let's go," Ty said as he started his car up. Nate and Lance jumped into their own car and was going to follow Ty. He had a long drive ahead of him and he had to figure out how he was going to approach Q. He sped off playing "I'll Whoop Your Head Boy" by rapper 50 Cent.

Q pulled up to the Cloverdale Warehouse and parked in the back. He closed his eyes as he thought about what was about to happen. *It's life or death, do or die* he said to himself. He stepped out of the car and checked the parking lot. No other activity seemed to be going on, and no other cars were in sight. He walked inside thinking he was the first one to make it there. He turned the lights on and did a security check. He had to double check that no one else was there.

After he felt secure, he went into the office booth and sat down. He double checked that he had his bullet proof vest on and was ready. He heard a car pulling up and knew it had to be Ty. He stepped out of the office and stood in the middle of the warehouse.

Ty walked inside with a smile on his face. "A rescheduled drop Q? Come on now, you couldn't do no better than that?" Ty got right to the point. He made it known to Q that he knew what time it was.

Q looked him in his face disgusted, "You couldn't be more than a snake nigga?" Q asked him while looking in his eyes.

"Fuck you Q! What the fuck makes you so special nigga?" Ty asked with hatred in his voice.

"Special? Special nigga? I didn't know your brother had to be special for you to be loyal," Q stated aggressively.

"Brother? Do you know what a brother is Q? Brothers don't act like their better than you, brothers don't deny helping another nigga out, you ain't my brother." Ty meant every word he spoke.

"Better than somebody Ty? How the fuck do you sound? Everybody around me eats. You seem to be the only nigga mad and hating. It's my fault you move the way you move? How many times have I told you to invest your money into something that can bring it back. *Everybody* has the same opportunities as me!" Q was screaming now, "And it wasn't my fucking job to help your cousin out nigga! You could have did that! I had to work to get to where I am, wasn't shit handed to me. Look around us Ty, everybody that's *around* has been *around*. You ever heard of no new niggas?!" Q was heated now. He couldn't believe Ty was really trying to justify him being foul.

"Man, fuck all that shit Q. It is what it is," Ty pulled his gun out and pointed it at Q. He looked him in his face, but he didn't budge or flinch.

"So that's how you gonna do me huh?" Q stated smirking. "You just gone rob me, fuck my bitch and then back out on me like this?" Q laughed. "Wow what a man!" he became serious again.

"Yeah, I ain't the only one that's gone back out tho," Ty said as the warehouse door opened and Nate walked in with his gun pointed.

Q snatched his gun from his back and shot at Nate first as he fired at the same time. Two of Q's bullets hit Nate, one in the chest and one in the stomach. He kept shooting while going down and hit Q three times in the chest. The hits caused Q to stumble. He had his vest on but the impact was still heavy. As he was stumbling back, he heard Kim call his name out. He thought he was just hearing things until he heard it again.

"Q!!!" Kim screamed. When he turned to look at her Ty shot him in the face. Q's body hit the ground in what seemed like slow motion to Kim.

"Nooooo! You motha fucka!" Kim said to Ty as she shot almost every bullet in her gun. Each hit made Ty's body shake. Kim watched as his blood spit out from the holes she was putting in his chest.

When Ty hit the ground, Kim walked up to his body and stood over him. So many emotions were running through her mind and her body was boiling hot. She watched as Ty struggled to breath as his mouth filled up with blood.

"Rot in hell motha fucka," was the last thing Kim said to him before she pulled the trigger and shot him in the face. Ty died with his eyes open, looking into Kim's.

She turned around shaking as she looked at Q's body on the floor. She kept her gun in her hand as she walked over to him slowly.

"Q! Baby! Oh my god!" she started to cry as she looked at his bloody body and face. She fell down to her knees and dropped her gun. She couldn't touch him; she couldn't even recognize him.

"Oh my god, why?! Q wake up baby please wake up," she was grabbing his shirt now. She knew he wasn't going to wake up but she still cried for him to. "I can't leave you like this Q, we gotta go baby get up! Come on get up!" Kim was losing her mind. She knew he was gone but she couldn't find it in her to leave him. She rocked back and forth over Q's body and cried until she heard sirens.

She looked around and thought about how she would explain these three dead bodies to the cops and her mind started racing. She looked down at Q. She wanted to kiss him, but his face was disfigured. She hated the fact that she had to leave him there.

"I love you baby. Say hi to Toya and save me a spot." She kissed her hand and touched his chest over his heart. Kim grabbed her gun and got up, ready to leave.

As she walked out of the warehouse, she was caught off guard and someone who must have been with Ty jumped out on her. He had his gun out and pointed as he looked confused to see a girl coming out. This gave Kim a little advantage over him as she shot first. She hit him in his shoulder and he shot back. Kim's stomach started burning as she looked down.

"*OH SHIT*!" she said as she held her stomach. Her shirt was slowly turning red as her body was burning. She looked up angry and shot the guy with her last bullet. It hit him in his chest, and he hit the ground.

Kim felt weak. She almost hit the ground but she fought against the pain. *I can't die here* she told herself as she looked around the parking lot. *I should go inside and die with Q*. Her mind was playing tricks on her now. *Do I wanna die? Do I deserve to live? Toya's dead, Q's dead, Ty's dead, maybe I'm supposed to go too.*

Kim felt weak again as she fell down on one knee. She grabbed her stomach, looked at the warehouse door and then looked at her car. She heard the sirens getting closer. She closed her eyes as she thought about her future, she wanted to live. She opened her eyes and stood up with all of her strength. She let out a shriek as she began to walk towards her car. She opened the door, slid in painfully, and started it up. She kept her lights off as she pulled out of the parking lot.

The freeway was right around the corner and she made it safely. She looked into her rearview mirror as she thought about what she just went through. After about 10 minutes of driving, she pulled over to check herself. She felt like she was bleeding more now that she was sitting down. It took all of her strength to get out of her car and make it to her trunk. She took out what seemed like a jacket and wrapped it around her stomach as tight as she could. She was no doctor but she knew pressure needed to be added to her wound. She prayed that it would last long enough for her to make it back to Q's private doctor.

Kim drove in silence as she was devastated. If she had any type of heart left in her it was gone now for sure. All she could do was cry as she replayed Q's body hitting the floor. She couldn't accept that Q was gone. She felt great being able to take Ty out, but she needed her man back. He was the last thing besides Momma that she had left in life with her. Ty set her up against her nigga and then killed him. That was her soulmate and Kim couldn't handle it.

Damn God, where the fuck is my happy ending? She thought to herself. *Wasn't taking Toya enough?* She cried as she questioned God. *What am I supposed to do now* is all she kept asking herself. She had her money, she had her stuff packed, and she had a place she could go to but she planned on having Q with her. The fact that she watched him die changed everything. She just wanted to go be with him and Toya whether it was heaven or hell. She felt like she had no reason to live anymore.

She knew she had to pull herself together, but she couldn't stop blaming herself for everything that had happened. She turned her radio on and *Oh-Ooh* child was playing just like it was when she told Q about Toya's death. She left it on this time and turned the volume all the way up. Her thoughts were taking over.

Oh-ooh child, things are gonna get easier.

Oh-ooh child, things are gonna get brighter.

Oh-ooh child, things are gonna get easier.

Oh-ooh child, things are gonna get brighter.

The music was pumping through her speakers. She wanted to turn it off but she couldn't find the strength. She missed Toya and Q so deeply she felt numb. She had no thoughts of where she was driving to, she was just driving. She replayed memories over in her head from times with her mother as a child to her mother's funeral. She remembered how she felt sitting in the front row looking at a woman in a casket who looked nothing like her mother.

After that day, she buried her feelings, her emotions, and her heart. She was lost without her mother. She cried harder now as the feelings came back to her. The words to the song made it easier for her tears to flow. Her memories went on to when she met Toya.

She remembered feeling cared about again. She felt like she had someone with her in the world now.

Kim cried and cried. Her thoughts went to Q, the only man she had ever truly given her heart to. Everyone she loved and cared about was gone.

Someday yeah…we'll put it together
And we'll get it all done.
Some day when your head is much lighter.

The song continued to play through Kim's car speakers. She continued to drive with no destination as she sang the words out loud.

Someday, yeah we'll walk in the rays of the
beautiful sun.

Some day when the world is much brighter.

Ooh-ooh child, things are gonna get easier.

Ooh-ooh child, things are gonna get brighter.

Ooh-ooh child, things are gonna get easier.

Ooh-ooh child, things are gonna get brighter.

Kim's eyes were blurry and burning. She looked up in her rearview mirror and saw that she was being followed. "Oh shit," she said out loud. She stepped on the pedal as she tried to go faster. The car sped up right behind her. Kim was nervous, she looked down at her stomach and saw she was bleeding through the sweater she wrapped around herself. She didn't know how much longer she had but she knew that time was running out. She started to feel dizzy as she drove faster and it caused her to slow down. *I'm dyin', oh my God, I'm dyin'* is all she could say to herself as her vision became blurry. She drove the car over towards the right, trying to pull over. She put the car in park and looked in the rearview. The car that was following her had pulled over with her. Kim wanted to cry but she couldn't, she was too weak. She had no energy to fight anymore. *It's over* is the last thing she said to herself as she closed her eyes, and everything went blank…

CHAPTER TWELVE

"Oh my god baby! Guess what?" Kim said as she jumped up and down in front of Q.

"What is it baby? Damn you actin' like a kid in a candy store," Q asked her as he smiled. He wanted to know what she was so excited about.

"I'm pregnant, were having a babyyy," Kim told Q as she wrapped her arms around his neck and jumped up to hug him. Q felt joy and happiness come over him.

"For real this time? You took the test babe? Let me see." Q was excited, but he wanted to make sure it was real this time. They'd been trying to conceive, and Kim had been having pregnancy scares.

He looked at the two dark pink lines on the test, it was official. He grabbed Kim and hugged her tightly. It was finally happening, and he'd been waiting for this day.

"I love you so much! I'm going to take care of you and our baby. This is all I ever wanted." Q meant every word he said as he smiled inside.

Kim almost let out a tear, "I love you so much more Q. If it's a girl, I wanna name her after Toya. If it's a boy, you know I'm making him a junior," she smiled as she thought about her future with Q. She kissed him on his lips as she looked him in his eyes and saw the love that he had for her. She never wanted to leave him again. The doorbell to their mansion rang and it startled her.

"Who could be coming to see us baby?" she asked Q as she walked to the huge glass door. "I don't know baby, maybe it's Momma," he answered saying the first person that came to his head.

As Kim opened the door, she saw a man in all black holding a bouquet of flowers. She smiled as she turned around to look at Q.

"Aww baby, are these for…" her sentence was cut short when she saw the look on Q's face. She turned around towards the door and the man holding the flowers was now holding a gun. He opened fire and shot Kim and Q with no hesitation.

Kim woke up screaming, but no sound came out. She was sweating and laying in a hospital bed with doctors surrounding her. She tried to speak again, and no sound came out. She raised her hand to try and catch one of the doctor's attention, but they seemed to be ignoring her. She couldn't understand why they were acting like she didn't exist. She tried to move and felt a horribly, sharp pain in her stomach. She lifted her hospital gown and saw her stomach was gauzed up and bleeding through. *Oh my gosh I'm going to bleed to death* she thought as the pain became worse.

She tried to get out of the bed and couldn't. The bleeding became worse and the doctors were still walking around her like she wasn't trying to get their attention.

"HELP ME!" she tried one more time to speak and this time her voice was heard. "Help me please!" she cried out again.

A doctor walked over to her with a long black lab coat on and a face mask as if the room was contagious.

"What can I do for you?" the doctor's voice gave Kim the chills. He sounded just like Ty.

"Doctor, I think I'm going to bleed to death." She ignored the fact that the doctor sounded like Ty. She thought her mind was just playing tricks on her.

"Let's take a look at it," the masked doctor said, again giving Kim the chills with his voice. Kim lifted her hospital gown up to show him. She looked up and saw that the doctor had taken his mask off. She almost fainted when she saw it was Ty. Instant tears fell from her eyes.

"What's wrong Kim? You look like you've seen a ghost," Ty was speaking sarcastically as he laughed.

Kim tried to scream but her voice was nonexistent again. Ty pulled a gun out and pointed it at Kim. She was still crying in silence as she looked around the hospital room and saw that now all of the other doctors were gone. It was just her and Ty. He took the gun and pushed it into her wound. Kim's stomach burned like someone lit it on fire. She screamed and screamed, but no sound came out. She was helpless. The pain was unbearable and she passed out looking Ty in the face as he smiled.

Kim woke up sweating again. *What the hell is going on*, she thought to herself. She looked around and she was still in a hospital room. This time she was on an operating table. She immediately lifted her hospital gown to check her stomach, she had no wound. She looked around the room and saw she was alone.

There was a hospital curtain covering a window. When she pulled it back, she saw Q laying on a hospital bed sound asleep. Kim banged on the window screaming, "Q baby, Q," but he didn't wake or budge. She turned around in a hurry, looking for a way out of the room. There were no doors and no other windows. *What the fuck kind of hospital is this*, she thought to herself. She continued to search for a way out to no avail. She gave up and decided she would try to break through the window that separated her and Q.

She grabbed one of the doctor's steel stools and went to hit the window. This time when she looked, she saw Ty walking into the room with Q while he was still asleep.

"No motha fucka!" Kim screamed out and once again her voice disappeared. She couldn't understand what was going on. She banged and banged on the glass with no success of breaking it. Ty went on as if he didn't hear or see Kim banging on the window.

Kim watched as he stood over Q's body, holding a gun. He wasted no time shooting him in the face.

"You motha fuckin' bastard! You piece of shit! You grimy ass son of a bitch," Kim went crazy. She was yelling, screaming and banging on the window. "I hate you! I fuckin' hate you, you snake ass motha fucka!" Kim continued on as if Ty could hear her. She watched with fury in her eyes as he left the room after shooting Q. She dropped to her knees and cried like a baby until she fell asleep.

"Kim, Kim, wake up," Toya whispered into Kim's ear. "Please wake up babe." Kim heard Toya's voice but she couldn't open her eyes. *I hear you T, keep talking*, Kim said to herself in her head with her eyes still closed. She couldn't open them.

"Kim, if you can hear me then listen. We need you to wake up. Q and I need you to pull through this. You're so strong and it's not your time to go. You are going to get over this little tattoo wound and pull through! We still need *more* time together," Toya said, still whispering in her ear. Tears fell from Kim's eyes, but she still couldn't open them. She tried to speak but her throat closed up. *I love you Toya. I hear you but I can't wake up. I wish you could hear me.*

Toya wiped Kim's tears. "You must hear me. That's right baby I have faith in you. You're the fighter, you're the strong one. Now don't you worry about me, don't you worry about Q, you worry about Kim and getting better." Toya kissed Kim on her cheek.

Don't go Toya, please don't leave me. I can't wake up, but I can hear you. I wish I could see your face. I'm gonna pull through, I've always been a fighter, I'm going to make it.

Kim spoke to herself in her head, reflecting on what Toya said. She tried to speak again and nothing came out. She tried to open her eyes and surprisingly they opened. She shut them quickly when she saw a bright white light. It was too bright for her eyes since they had been closed for a while.

"She's waking up. Quick call the doctor! She's trying to open her eyes," Kim heard Toya say to someone. She tried to open her eyes again, this time slowly. She squinted and she saw Toya's beautiful face smiling at her. More tears fell from Kim's eyes. She tried to reach out to her friend, but she started to fade away as if she was leaving.

"Wait Toya come back, don't go," Kim was able to speak and hear herself. Toya turned around and smiled at Kim. She had her pointer finger over her lips as if she was telling her to hush. Kim was confused. She wanted her friend to come back.

"Come back Toya! Come back!" Kim yelled and screamed.

"Hello Ms. Carter. I am Doctor Z. You have been shot *really* badly and you're in shock. Please calm down and let me work on you. There's no Toya here it's you, my team and I. We are going to do our very best to get you well," Dr. Z told Kim as best he could through her screams and cries.

"Just let me die! Just leave me alone and let me die! I can't do this shit anymore. Let me die!" Kim cried out.

"Ok we have to sedate her. There's no way we'll be able to do anything to her while she's in this state,"

Dr. Z told one of his team members. He looked down at Kim as she fell back out of consciousness…

Two weeks Later

Frankie stood next to Dr. Z and watched Kim as she slept. Her body would jump here and there as if she was having nightmares and she even cried in her sleep. Frankie wondered what she was dreaming about as he admired her. Her face was looking much better now and her bruises were healing well. He felt sorry for what he had done to her, but he knew that he was only following his boss's orders as always. He was doing everything he could now to take care of Kim as he knew Q would have wanted him to do.

Before meeting with Ty, Q asked Frankie to be his eyes behind his head. This is how he was able to save Kim. He wasn't too far behind all the commotion that was going on at the warehouse. He just wished he could have saved Q in time. He didn't expect Kim to be there, so when he saw her, he had to rearrange his plans. He had gotten her to Q's private doctor just in time for him to stitch her up before she bled out. The bullet had entered her side just above her right hip, traveled upward and lodged itself into her lower rib cage. Luckily for Kim, the 9mm that she was shot with carried bullets that stayed intact rather than splitting into pieces after hitting or entering the body.

After going through two surgeries, they both thought it was best to keep her heavily sedated during the first week or so of recovery. The bullet was still in her and it was too risky trying to remove it. Her recovery was going to be painful.

"She's very lucky to be alive," Dr. Z told Frankie. "People who get shot where she did often times do not make it," he continued. "She's going to have a long recovery, especially in the state that she's in," he advised. Dr. Z had given Kim her last dose and she was due to wake up any time now.

"I want to watch her vital signs for the next hour or so before I leave her," Dr. Z said, concerned. He traveled for the right price and he was beyond loyal to Q. He traveled back and forth to be with Kim as he had other patients who needed him also. He was getting ready to travel back to Long Island that evening.

"Now when she wakes up, she may seem a little confused and out of it. This girl has been through a lot but I know she'll do just fine. Make sure you give her all of her medications around the clock. It's very important that she stays on her antibiotics to avoid an infection. She still has an open wound on her." Dr. Z spoke very clear and serious to Frankie.

He was leaving her in his care and wouldn't be back for a week or so when it was time to check up on her. He wanted Kim to arise from this horrible accident. He was deeply saddened by what happened to Q. Dr. Z had been his doctor for over a decade and Q had always been one of his favorite patients.

"Do not worry doctor, I am a man of my word and I will take great care of her," he assured Dr. Z.

"Okay then. Her vitals seem to be stable. I'll be heading off now. *DO NOT* hesitate to call me if you need me," Dr. Z emphasized. He was only one call away. Frankie gave him a hand shake before he left the room.

As Kim woke up, she looked around with her eyes fast and confused. She had no idea where she was and she started to freak out. She felt a tube in her nose and it was uncomfortable. She wanted to rip it out but her arms were too weak. She felt her eyes watering up but she didn't know what she was crying for. She looked over to her left and saw the same man from before sitting there. *What the fuck? Am I kidnapped again? Am I dreaming again?* She asked herself in her head. She wanted to move but she couldn't, she started breathing heavily and her eyes were overflowing with water now.

"It's ok, I am not going to hurt you anymore. You have my word miss lady," Frankie said to Kim as he stood over her and rubbed her arm. His voice was so sincere. It didn't sound the way it did when Kim was tied to a chair.

She almost felt like she could trust him. She calmed down a little and started breathing easier. For some reason she still couldn't talk or control her emotions. She just looked at Frankie and cried as she turned her head, closed her eyes, and went right back to sleep.

Frankie stood over Kim and thought about how he watched her heal for the past two weeks. She had come a very long way. He reminisced about how weak her body was when he took her out of her car. She had blood everywhere and anybody would have automatically assumed she was dead.

Dr. Z was already on standby which was one of Q's orders. He wanted to be ready at all times and he knew the chances of him being shot were high. He was prepared for himself and ended up saving Kim's life.

Frankie drove as fast as he could to get Kim to Dr. Z's and Kim unconsciously held his hand the whole way. He promised Q that he would hold Kim down if anything was to happen to him and he did just that. The police were close before he got to her. He could have walked away and left her after seeing Q go down, but he didn't. Frankie has always been a man of his word. He felt guilty about not being able to save Q in time, but he felt a little better knowing that he saved the next best thing to him, Kim. He knew that this had to count for something up in heaven to Q.

He called Dr. Z just to let him know that she had woke up for a few minutes. He knew it was normal but he still wanted to keep him updated with everything.

After getting off the phone, he went back into the room to be with Kim.

Frankie did everything the doctor told him to do. Hours had passed by now and Kim was still asleep. He watched Kim as she turned her head from side to side. She seemed like she was trying to wake up but couldn't. He continued to watch as she eventually opened her eyes. She looked around as if it was her first time waking up. She seemed confused again like she had no idea where she was.

"It's ok miss lady, I'm not going to hurt you," Frankie reassured her again that everything was okay. Kim tried to speak but the words wouldn't come out. She tried again, taking her time.

"Where," she stopped and swallowed "where am I?" she asked with all her strength. She looked around again, worried.

"You're in a safe place. The doctor that Q took you to before is the same one that stitched you up and saved your life miss lady," Frankie said, answering her question.

"Q," Kim said before crying again.

Frankie rubbed her arm, "Calm down miss lady, you are going to be fine. If you're in any pain let me know."

Kim just looked at Frankie. She was confused as to why he was being so nice to her, but she had no energy to spark a conversation. She was able to say three words, the most before her body started feeling like it was using too much strength. She told Frankie she was in pain as he instructed her to do and he brought her medicine right away. He was at her every call. She appreciated Frankie although she still had sour feelings towards him for what he had done to her. He saved her life so she couldn't hate him that much. Now Frankie was basically all she had.

She felt as if the pain medicine had kicked in. It worked quickly being administered into her IV, and it felt great. She felt like she was floating on clouds, and all she could do was think.

Q was gone and Toya was gone. She had to figure out her next move. She wondered how long she would be as helpless as she felt. She was thankful to be alive but the pain of being alone was unbearable. She hated that this strange man had to take care of her. She wanted to get over this wound and be herself again.

She wondered if she could trust Frankie. She had no idea where her car was and it held all she had left, her money. She thought about her apartment, *how will I get the rest of my things now*? She thought about trusting Frankie again. She didn't know how long it would be until she was able to move around and she needed her belongings.

Her eyes became heavy as her thoughts went on. She thought about Momma Margaret. She wondered if she knew what happened to Q. She thought about Q more, she wondered if he had a funeral and if it was open casket. *Did everybody see him like that?* she thought to herself. She closed her eyes as memories flashed in her head of Q's face being blown off and his body hitting the ground. She hated the fact that she had these horrible memories while awake and even more horrible nightmares when she was asleep. She wondered when they would stop. Her thoughts and dreams wouldn't allow her to miss her friends in peace. Her thoughts drifted off as the medicine took over her body and she fell back to sleep.

Frankie turned the lights out and sat in the dark. He opened his nightstand drawer and took out his stress balls. He twirled them around in his hand as he watched Kim sleep and his thoughts wandered. He knew the love her and Q had for each other was real and he respected it. He wondered what was going to happen after Kim fully recovered. Now that Q was gone, a lot of things were going to change. He has been beyond loyal to Q and although he didn't expect payment in return, he wanted some kind of recognition. He thought about Q, *such a loyal boss* he said to himself. He looked over at Kim again while still moving his stress relievers around in his

hands and he smiled, *there's a new boss in town now...*

THE END!

Made in the USA
Middletown, DE
30 September 2023